About the Author

Magenta is the pen name of a dreamer. One who enjoys all the smutty deliciousness romance can bring. One who knows how much real life can bring you down and knows the value of being able to escape into a pretend world. Pretend worlds, where there is always a happy ever after.

Also by Magenta

Arbor Vitae Coven

(Paranormal Romance Series)

Candy Conniptions

Dreamy Delights

Fangs and Fireworks

Christmas Capers

(Coming 2023)

Fangs and Fireworks

ARBOR VITAE COVEN
BOOK THREE

MAJENTA

Fangs and Fireworks
Mobi format: : 978-0-6487006-8-5
Print: 978-0-6487006-9-2

Cover design by Dazed Designs
Edited by Elemental Editing

This one's for you Jess. Thank you for all your words of support they mean everything to me.

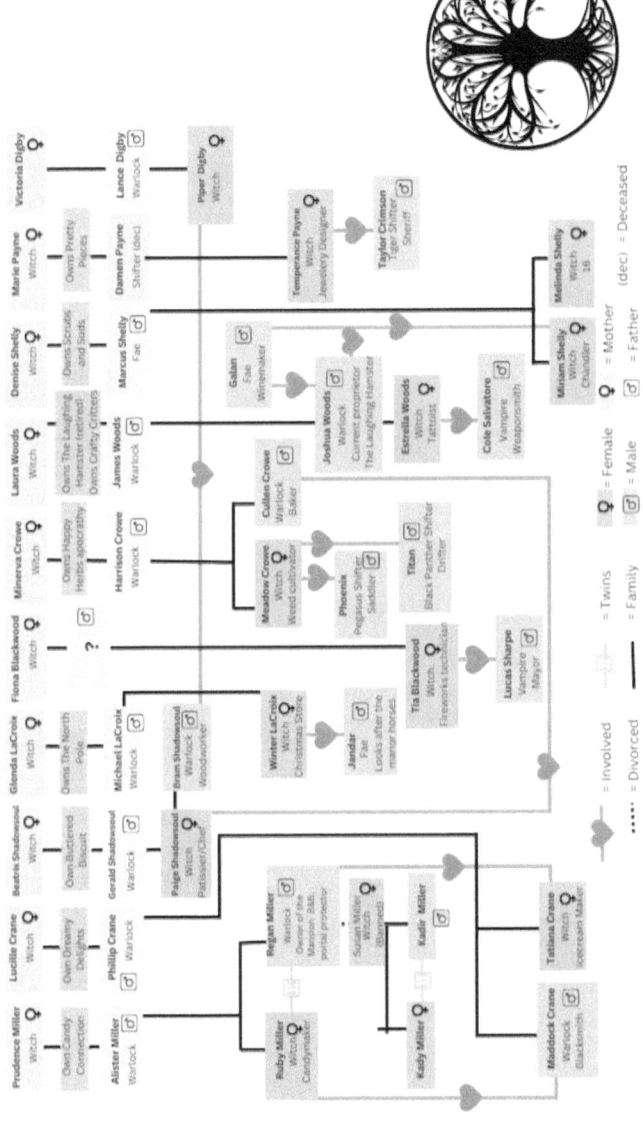

♀ = Female
♂ = Male
(dec) = Deceased
♀ = Mother
♂ = Father
= Twins
= Family
= Involved
= Divorced

Victoria Digby ♀
Lance Digby ♂ Warlock
Piper Digby ♀ Witch

Marie Payne ♀ Witch — Owns Pretty Pieces
Damen Payne ♂ Shifter (dec)
Temperance Payne ♀ Witch — Jewellery Designer
Taylor Crimson ♂ Tiger Shifter — Sheriff

Denise Shelly ♀ Witch — Owns Scrubs and Suds
Marcus Shelly ♂ Fae

Laura Woods ♀ Witch — Owns The Laughing Hamster (retired) Owns Crafty Critters
James Woods ♂ Warlock

Minerva Crowe ♀ Witch — Owns Happy Herbs apiocathy
Harrison Crowe ♂ Warlock

Fiona Blackwood ♀ Witch
?

Glenda LaCroix ♀ Witch — Owns The North Pole
Michael LaCroix ♂ Warlock

Beatrix Shadowsoul ♀ Witch — Own Buttered Biscuit
Gerald Shadowsoul ♂ Warlock

Lucille Crane ♀ Witch — Own Dreamy Delights
Phillip Crane ♂ Warlock

Prudence Miller ♀ Witch — Own Candy Connection
Alster Miller ♂ Warlock

Gadan ♂ Fae — Winemaker
Joshua Woods ♂ Warlock — Current proprietor The Laughing Hamster
Estrella Woods ♀ Witch — Tattoos
Cole Salvatore ♂ Vampire — Weaponsmith
Miriam Shelly ♀ Witch — Chandler
Melinda Shelly ♀ Witch — 16

Cullen Crowe ♂ Warlock — Baker
Meadow Crowe ♀ Witch — Weed cultivator
Phoenix ♀ Pegasus Shifter — Saddler
Titan ♂ Black Panther Shifter — Drifter

Winter LaCroix ♀ Witch — Christmas Store
Jandar ♂ Fae — Looks after the manor horses

Paige Shadowsoul ♀ Witch — Retriever/Clerk
Brian Shadowsoul ♂ Warlock — Woodworker

Tia Blackwood ♀ Witch — Fireworks technician
Lucas Sharpe ♂ Vampire — Mayor

Regan Miller ♂ Warlock — Owner of the Mansion B&B, portal protector
Susan Miller ♀ Witch (banjoed)
Kadie Miller ♂
Ruby Miller ♀ Witch — Candymaker
Kadry Miller ♀
Tatiana Crane ♀ Witch — Icecream Maker
Maddock Crane ♂ Warlock — Blacksmith

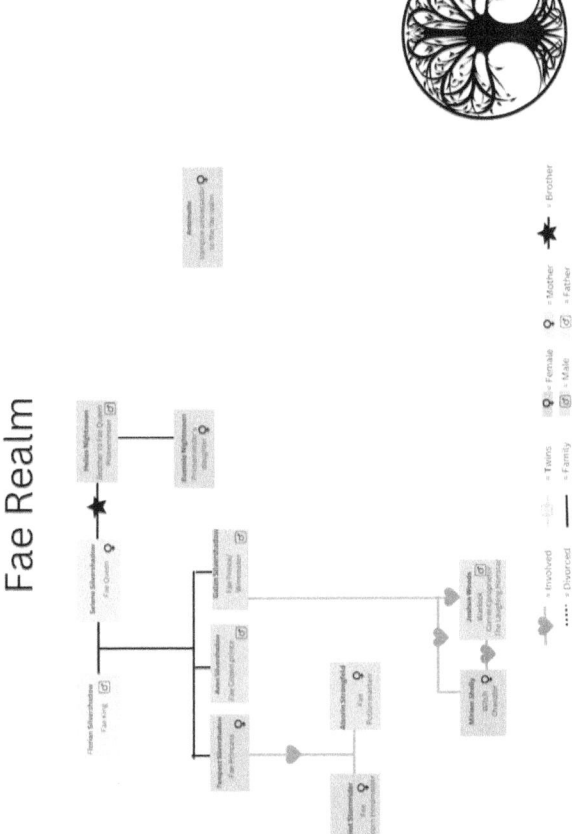

Fae Realm

Vampire Realm

Prologue

T he weather in LA is a lot warmer than Morbank Island when Tatiana and Ruby's plane touches down, and the smell of airplane exhaust permeates the chilly air.

It's early morning, but the sky is already a clear, bright blue, so it should warm up as the day progresses.

They pick up their rental SUV from the counter at the airport and plug Meadow's last known address into the GPS.

"What did Minerva say when you asked about Meadow's whereabouts?" Tatiana asks Ruby as she steers the SUV into the early morning traffic.

"She said Meadow had been in Amsterdam for about a year, but she's now living in LA. She also said there is a possibility she is up north in Eureka. The company she is working for has a marijuana farm up there, but they have retail stores in LA and San Francisco, so she could be anywhere." Ruby's gaze stays on the busy road, but Tatiana can tell that she's rolling her eyes. Their friend Meadow is a little flaky.

"And what about Tia?"

"Fiona said Tia has been all over the world. She was so hurt and angry when Mr. Lee wouldn't teach her the family business," Ruby replies.

"I remember. She said, 'Screw him, I'll learn from someone else.'" Tatiana thinks for a moment. "That was just after graduation. She and Estella were the first to leave, remember? The rest of us didn't until a couple years later."

"She kept in touch with Fiona at first. It must have been before the spell was cast, and they talked all the time. She spent a long time in Australia, learning from one of the great pyrotechnic dynasties there, but then the communication slowly dissipated." Ruby shouts some words of abuse at an LA motorist and gives them the finger before continuing. "The only reason she knows where she's been is because she was able to track her with locator spells. Tia went to anyone who would give her a chance. The Lee name gave her an in, and most of them weren't sexist old coots like her grandpa. The last locator spell showed her here in LA, and all it took to find her was googling a few pyrotechnic companies and asking if she worked there." Ruby sounds smug over her detective skills.

"Thank goodness. I thought she might have been in China," Tatiana replies.

They remain quiet as the busy city of LA passes them on their way to their first stop.

Ruby eventually pulls the SUV into a parking bay not far from the dispensary where Meadow is supposedly working. High Hopes is located in an older area that has recently been revitalized, the aged warehouses turned into funky little boutique-style retail stores and cafes.

The words "High Hopes" are painted in neon green, graffiti-style writing in big, bold letters across the front. Nobody can miss the two-story corner building, and it seems to be popular with locals.

Music floats out of the cafe doors as Tatiana and Ruby walk toward the dispensary. There are a lot of people around for early morning—the uniqueness of the area a draw for tourists and locals alike.

As they get closer, the skunky, earthy smell of weed drifts to their nostrils, and both breathe it in and turn to each other with smiles. Tatiana shakes her head, and Ruby's lips turn down in a pout. "No, we don't have time. Let's get in and find Meadow and then be on our way to get Tia. The mayor needs us back as soon as possible if we are going to organize Feast and Fireworks for Thanksgiving."

They enter the store, which has classic Bob Marley playing over the speakers. The large, open windows allow plenty of light and fresh air to stream into the store, and the eye-catching displays of various cannabis options draw the gaze and tempt the patron. A man who looks to be in his mid-twenties greets the girls as they approach the counter. His faux-hawk is gelled to within an inch of its life and colored a bright neon blue. His eyebrow has a bar through it, drawing attention to his warm chocolate eyes that seem quite clear for someone who works in this kind of business. Maybe it's still too early for him.

"Good morning, ladies. What can I tempt you with today?" His tone is mellow and smooth and could probably tempt you to buy almost anything.

"Hi, we're looking for Meadow." Ruby's voice is bright and friendly, and so is her smile. "Is she here?"

His eyes dim slightly, and he shakes his head. "No, sorry, lovely, but Meadow is up north at the farm at the moment. They had a crisis with a new strain she helped develop, so she flew up there to help out. She won't be back for a week or so."

The girls look at each other in disappointment, thank the guy, then leave.

"Well, crap," Tatiana grumbles as she exits the store. "What now?"

"Don't stress. We're zero for one, but we still have Tia. Let's go get her, and then we can shoot up north and get Meadow." Jumping back into the car, they plug the address into the GPS and head for Tia's workplace.

Over an hour later, they pull into the parking lot for one of the most famous pyrotechnic companies in LA. Well known for its special effects and large-scale productions, FF Productions is housed in a large warehouse in an industrial area of LA.

Tatiana looks around. "Surely they don't make them here. It seems like too much of a risk with all these other buildings around."

Ruby's eyes follow the same path, and she shrugs. "It's probably just storage. It doesn't look fancy enough to be a display room, so I guess this is where all the planning happens."

They ring the doorbell set into the wall of the large concrete building and wait for someone to answer. A young girl, probably in her late teens, responds, looking a little confused to see people at the door.

"Can I help you?" she asks warily.

"Hi, we're looking for Tia Blackwood," Tatiana replies. "We were told she works here."

"Yeah, she does, but she's not here," the girl says and goes to shut the door, but Ruby sticks her foot in the frame.

"Do you know when she will be back?" Ruby's voice holds a hint of steel and impatience.

The girl rolls her eyes. "They are all up at the Toronto International Fireworks Festival. They won't be back for a few weeks." Ruby moves her foot as she gapes at Tatiana in shock, and the girl manages to slam the door shut.

"Shit, she's practically on our back doorstep." Tatiana groans while Ruby's brain goes into planning mode.

She starts to head toward the car with Tatiana following. "Right, new plan now that we're zero for two."

They climb in and head back toward the airport.

"We'll go up to Eureka and grab Meadow, and then we'll head home and nab Tia on the way." Ruby nods her head in determination, and Tatiana just laughs.

"You're the boss." She leans back in her seat and observes Ruby's fiercely determined, but downright dangerous, driving all the way back to the airport.

CHAPTER
One

Tia

The smell of gunpowder permeates the air as the smoke drifts lazily across the river. The bright fireworks in the sky reflect on the mirror-like surface in front of me, and the loud bangs as they explode, followed by the echoing cheers from the crowd, bring a huge grin to my face. I am living the dream doing what I've always wanted to do. A couple of colleagues pat me on my back, congratulating me, and I get respectful head nods from some of the competitors.

The Toronto International Fireworks Competition is a world-class competition where the competitors are the best of the best from each of their respective countries and companies, and here, I am holding my own amongst them all. The grin that spreads across my face is so wide, it hurts. I'm finally proving what I've been telling *him* all along, and I didn't even need to use magic to achieve it.

My smile dims slightly at the thought of magic. I push a stray tendril of hair behind my ear as I think about the last time I used it. Hmm, I push the thought aside as the soundtrack comes to an end and the crowd bursts into rapturous applause after the finale of my display. The gathered people start to disperse, since mine was the last display of the night, and my crew and I start the tedious job of breaking everything down so that the next team can set up in the morning.

"Nice job, Tia," someone with an Australian accent calls from somewhere, and I wave my hand in the general direction of the voice but don't stop what I'm doing. It's been a busy couple of days, and now I'm ready for a break. I want a hot bath and a glass of wine before climbing into my lovely, comfortable hotel bed.

Wires are disconnected and rewound, and launch setups are broken down and stored in boxes. The control panel is placed carefully into the padded box, ready to be shipped back to LA in a couple of days.

"That was amazing, Tia, and it went off without a hitch. Congratulations!"

I look up and find the owners of FF grinning at me, their arms wrapped around each other. Jonathan and Sable Edwards have become some of my closest friends since I came to LA, and we share a three-way hug as we jump up and down like school children.

"If that doesn't win the competition for us, I'm not sure what will." Sable's husky voice can't contain her excitement, but Jonathon, the more sensible of the three of us, is quick to calm us down.

"Let's not count our chickens before they are hatched, okay? Let's be quietly confident so if we don't win, we won't look silly. Let's go have a drink to warm up. It's freezing out here." Jonathan stomps his feet and rubs his gloved hands together.

It's early November, but winter is already raising its frosty head. I get a pang of nostalgia as I think about home and whether they have had the first snow of winter yet. It was usually around Halloween, and my girlfriends and I would find somewhere to hangout after trick-or-treating and giggle and gossip while drinking whatever bottle of spirits one of us managed to steal from our parents' stash.

Never me, though, because my grandfather probably would have killed me if he caught me with a bottle of alcohol. I shudder, not wanting to think about that man right now, not when I'm enjoying a highlight of my career.

"Yeah, you guys go ahead, and I'll meet you in the hotel bar. I just have a few more things to square away."

They wave goodbye and warn me not to take too long before disappearing into the crowd. People are slow to make their way home despite the cold. It's a beautiful evening, and there are lots of food vendors and stalls for people to spend their hard-earned dollars on before returning to the comfort of their homes.

Looking around, I see my crew has all of our things except for the final case at my feet, so I lift it up. It's got some weight to it, and I struggle with it slightly. I'm not a big person, and sometimes the equipment does get the better of me.

I'm puffing with exertion, my breath foggy in the

cold air, as I make my way to the truck we hired. The stacks of people don't make it easy, and I have to use both hands to keep hold of the heavy case. I stop for a moment and lean against a tree, placing the case at my feet. After sucking in a couple of breaths, I pick it up again, and this time it practically flies into the air like it weighs nothing. I stumble backward, and a stranger's hand presses against my back, steadying me. I thank him for his help before glaring down at the case in my hands.

"Well, isn't that typical Tia, always having to do things the hard way," a voice drawls sarcastically behind me.

I whirl and eye the pink-haired girl leaning against the tree. "You know very well why I don't like to use my magic," I snap at my friend. I haven't seen her in years, and seeing her now makes my heart race and my hands shake.

"Yeah, but the old coot isn't around to pick on you, so I say screw him."

"You know, it's funny, I haven't used my magic in years. I haven't needed it, and I don't miss it, but this would have been a very handy spell over the years." I point at the case, which I dropped in my surprise. The damn thing is hovering just above the ground, and if I moved, it would follow behind me just like a puppy. The girls used to use the spell with our school bags all the time.

The pink-haired girl steps away from the tree and out into the light. Ruby practically glows with vibrancy. I'm almost certain if I could do the spell to reveal it, her aura would tell me so many things.

"You know you're not an easy woman to track down. The locator spell I did told us you were in LA. Imagine my surprise when we got there and found out you were practically in our backyard." She crosses her arms and gives me a classic Ruby look. It's one that's half disappointment, half concern. It's also one I'm very familiar with. I'm almost certain I'm the only one of the ten of us who was constantly on the receiving end of that look. "Were you even going to stop in and say hi?"

I cross my own arms in defense. "You know I wasn't, and you know the reason why. I have no reason to return to that island. My witch powers were practically nonexistent as a teenager, and I guarantee they haven't gotten any better. My mother was disinterested, and my grandfather was downright abusive—he was just skilled enough to hide it from the rest of the coven. I'm not sure what made the man so bitter or if it was just his own upbringing."

Ruby sighs and drops her arms. "Well, let's not worry about all that now. I'm so happy to see you." She engulfs me in her warm embrace. The familiar smell of sugar envelops me, and I'm instantly transported back to happier days. I used to hang out with my best buds at coven meetings we were still too young to attend, but then during our own induction into the coven, I was horrified to learn that I have no magic, or it's so diluted I can barely craft a fire spell.

In fact, that was about the only one I managed to master, and mostly because I thought it would be helpful when my grandfather finally let me into the family business, but no. My lack of magic finally sealed the coffin in that. Never has a Lee been so untalented.

He blamed it on my mother and my nonexistent father —a drifter warlock she made the mistake of having a drunken fling with, or so he used to tell me on a regular basis. He has never forgiven her for ruining the Lee family. He insisted that they marry, but my dear old dad didn't stick around, and he was gone before they could walk down the aisle.

I choke on a sob but bring my arms up to return her hug before pulling away. "What are you doing here, Rubes?" I ask, picking up the suitcase and carrying it the rest of the way to the truck. Ruby steps up beside me, shoving her hands deep into her pockets. The area has cleared slightly with the people moving farther down the street to the entertainment.

When we get to the truck, Travis is waiting.

"I thought you had gotten lost, Tia," he jokes, taking the case from my hand.

He was expecting it to be heavy, so he just about smacks himself in the face with it. I see Ruby murmur a spell, and it quickly returns to its former weight. Travis grunts as it gets heavier, but he almost has it into the truck.

He frowns. "Shit, maybe I had too many beers," he mutters, looking between his hands and the case, and Ruby smothers a giggle.

I huff and shove Travis toward the driver's side, knowing full well he doesn't drink on the job.

"Get all of that back to the storage unit. Jonathan has arranged for all of it to be transported back to LA tomorrow afternoon."

"Ah, yeah, sure. Goodnight and great job, Tia." He's still a little distracted as he climbs into the cab. I just hope he doesn't get lost on the way back to the storage unit.

Sighing, I face my old friend. "So is there a reason you are here, or am I just lucky?" I'm tired, and I really want to have a drink to celebrate my show, but I have a sinking feeling this is not just a casual visit.

"What? Can't a girl just want to see an old friend?" Ruby tries to pull off a casual response, but I know her too well, and I can see the worry in her eyes that she can't hide. I raise an eyebrow, and she grimaces. "Fine, I have a lot to tell you. Let's grab a drink, because this is definitely going to need at least one or two."

I sigh and pull out my phone. I send a text to my bosses, telling them I ran into an old friend and I'd take a rain check for that drink. Though, again, I have another funny feeling that may be a long time coming.

"Okay, I'll hear you out, but I don't like your chances if you want me to return home. If I never see that island again, it won't be soon enough."

Ruby sighs and brushes a strand of pink hair off her face. "I really hope you don't feel that way, because it needs you, and so do we."

We find a small but busy bar close by, and lucky for us, there's an empty booth. I grab it while Ruby gets us both a drink. When she slides in and passes it to me, I take a long sip, drinking almost half of it in one go. God knows I need the fortification if we're going to talk about the place I dread. Although I loved my friends and being a part of the coven, my home life sucked so badly that it far outweighed the good, but I couldn't actually tell anyone. My grandfather spelled me not to be able to talk about it. If I even put a toe out of line, he would punish me, and he would be creative. I'm pretty sure I still have indents on my knees from kneeling on raw rice on the wooden floor in his office.

I believe my mother's indifference was from a spell as well, but that didn't make it hurt any less. I'm not even sure she was aware of it. She moved through her days in a fog, and when she was with the coven, my grandfather manipulated her like a puppet so no one was any wiser, and I couldn't tell anyone about it.

The tale Ruby tells me does tug at the heartstrings, and I'm so happy to hear about her and Maddock, and Regan and Tatiana—like that wasn't a given. The rest of the children of the coven already had that pegged, but there was a running bet about how long it would take. If I see Josh, I'll have to ask him what the latest figures are and if anyone got close.

When I hear about the malaise that seems to be affecting everyone, I'm indifferent. "I don't know, Ruby. Maybe it didn't actually affect me because I have so little magic. I haven't felt any different from when I first left the island."

She chews on the straw sticking out of her cocktail, and I can see her thinking things over. "Still no magic?"

"Nope, I'm practically human, but I guess I haven't even noticed it was missing."

She waves a hand. "I hadn't noticed either, it's part of the spell. Nothing bad has happened to you in the last few weeks? The mothers did the spell about a month ago now."

I think about the last month and shake my head. "No, everything has been perfect. I don't know if you saw the show, but I nailed it. It has a real chance of winning."

"I did, and it was awesome. You deserve it. You can really stick it to the old coot now. He refused to train you, and now you're probably better trained than him. The only extra thing he has is magic, but the bastard has refused to do the fireworks display for the Thanksgiving feast. He flat-out slammed the door in Mayor Sharpe's face. The prejudiced bastard told him to take his bloodsucking fangs elsewhere." A sly look crosses her face, and she narrows her eyes on me.

"Even if you don't want to stay, it would really be sticking it to the old man if you came and helped out with Feast and Fireworks. He would blow a fuse."

My heart skips a beat at Ruby's words. Normally I'm not a petty person, but the thought of sticking it to my grandpa is probably just enough to get me to do what she wants. Before I can reply, she leans over and pours something into my cocktail from a golden flask that appeared on the table, followed by a tall purple flask.

"Hey, what was that?" I demand, eyeing my drink, and she shrugs.

"Just a potion, actually two. One to boost your magic after unuse, and another to counteract the malignant spell. Can't hurt you to have either even if you think you are unaffected."

"Fine, but when I drink this and nothing changes, I don't want you to argue with me when I decide to leave the island again. You have to let me go," I bargain, and she sighs.

"Fine, Tia, if you want to leave Morbank after Feast

and Fireworks, I won't fight you on it. But if your magic improves when you return, you have to promise to stay and help with the final spell before you leave again."

I hold out a hand, and we shake on it before I throw my drink back. I shudder at the taste as it works its way into my body. I see Ruby smile somewhat cunningly, and I have a moment of worry. I probably should have questioned her a little more about what the spells were. It's a little late now, though, so I'll just have to wait and say, "I told you so," once nothing happens. I will be counting down the days.

CHAPTER
Two

Lucas

Banging on the door of the house isn't getting any results. Just like the last two times I'd been to visit Mr. Lee, he is refusing to see me. His daughter, Fiona, is also absent. I haven't had the pleasure to meet her yet, since she's always been absent at any coven event I've attended in the past. I don't even think I know what she looks like.

"Fuck," I mutter under my breath as I give up. Last time I was here, I learned that if I don't give up, he'll start shooting fireworks at me, and the man has deadly aim. His magic also makes those fireworks a little more interesting than good old human ones. Last time, a dragon bit me on the ass before exploding in my face. Thank fuck for vampire healing. I needed two blood bags to get myself right after that little episode. Sure, I could have had him charged with assault, but that's not going to get the man to do my fireworks display for me on Thanksgiving.

Turning my back to the wooden door, I take the stairs down to the gravel driveway and step back, using my advanced senses to hear if anyone is around. The Blackwood/Lee household is slightly out of town with no houses nearby. Even though he uses magic, Mr. Lee still makes his fireworks the old-fashioned way with gunpowder and additives, and it wouldn't be safe for others to live too close by just in case of an accident.

As I listen, nothing but the sounds of a few birds, which haven't flown south for the winter, and the gentle rush of the wind through the dying trees greet my ears. I look around. For witches who are supposed to have an affinity with nature, I see no evidence here. Everything looks half dead. Even at the beginning of winter, there should be some sign of life, but there isn't. It's sad and depressing, and it fits Mr. Lee perfectly.

Huffing out a frustrated sigh, I head back into town. I thought about driving out here, but I chose to use my vampire speed and run, knowing I was probably going to be frustrated by the visit. Sure enough, I need the run back to the office too.

By the time I step into my office, I've calmed down from the irritation caused by going out there. I don't have a secretary, but the old basset hound I adopted when I was first elected to the mayor's position two years ago looks up as I arrive in a whoosh. He's so used to it now, he barely even blinks before closing his eyes again.

"Some guard dog you are, Buddy." I reach down and rub between his ears, and he grunts and rolls onto his back in bliss. Sighing, I throw myself into my comfortable leather chair and stair at the open fire across from my desk that Buddy has made himself comfortable in front of. It hisses and sparks and warms the room to a comfortable temperature. The first snow happened on Halloween last week, and it's only going to get colder. I need to make sure we have plenty of heating for Feast and Fireworks.

Picking up a pen, I add that to the huge list that is currently consuming all of my focus. The manor's Halloween haunted house was a huge success, and I want to capitalize on that and keep the momentum going with our Thanksgiving celebration. I've already lined up the entertainment and secured a huge supply of turkey legs, as well as a caterer who specializes in Thanksgiving feasts. Next, I need to lock in the tables and chairs. The coven's new community space only just started construction and won't be ready before Thanksgiving. Instead, I'm going to block off Main Street and set everything up along there, overlooking the river, and my idea was that a barge could be anchored for the fireworks, but Mr. Lee refuses to even open the door, let alone discuss it with me. I don't know what I'm going to do. We only have about three weeks left, and I very much doubt I'm going to be able to secure someone in time.

Ruby waltzed through here, reassuring me she has it under control, but she left the island on the second, and it's now the sixth, and she still hasn't returned. Tatiana arrived back yesterday with a pretty bubbly blond whom I saw go into Happy Herbs. There was screaming and crying, and I turned and went in the other direction. Family drama is not my thing. I have enough of that back in the vampire realm, but I think I may have picked the wrong place on Earth to set down roots, because there has been nothing but drama. Pru tells me it's due to a spell, which I still find a little hard to believe, but the woman is a force of nature, and who am I to get in her way? As long as she's actively helping the town, I have no problem with any of her schemes. My biggest worry has been the portal. There has been a rumble in the supernatural council about relocating it, saying that the Arbor Vitae Coven and Morbank Island aren't doing a good enough job of protecting or powering it. It's a load of shit, but now we need to prove it, hence Feast and Fireworks. We need the human and supernatural tourists to return in droves, and that is only one of my plans.

Thankfully, Christmas is always a big thing on Morbank. The North Pole Christmas store is hugely popular, and people come from miles around to see it. The LaCroix family—the owners—spend a good percentage of the year overseas, securing one of a kind artisan ornaments and decorations, but maybe we can add decorating and lighting a town tree to the calendar as well. We could serve cider and chestnuts and marshmallows roasting over an open fire. I'm sure the coven could grow me an oversized Christmas tree, especially after I saw how quickly they grew the corn maze. I make a note at the bottom of my list to speak to Pru about it next time I see her.

The outside door opens, and I hear someone come through it. "Lucas?" a male voice calls, and when he sticks his head through my open door, I see it's the sheriff.

"Hey, Taylor, come on in." He has his hat in hand, and he slaps it against his thigh before bending down and giving Buddy a rub between the ears. Buddy barely moves.

"You should think about getting yourself a receptionist," he says when he stands up to his full height.

"I don't really need one. It isn't like I'm run off my feet," I tell him, gesturing to a chair.

"Hopefully that changes soon." He places his hat on my desk before dropping his body into the chair.

"So what do I owe the pleasure?" I ask the tiger shifter. Taylor was one of the first townspeople I met when I moved to Morbank Island from the vampire realm. I needed a change, and this was a good compromise. It got me away from vampire politics, which I hated, and still gave me contact with the supernatural population. Here, I don't have to hide what I am, and even though supes are out, we're still a novelty and often feared.

Taylor sighs and runs a hand through his hair. Taylor's hair is sandy blond, but he has darker blond stripes similar to his tiger stripes dotted throughout. "I hate to be the bearer of bad news, but I just got a report of a missing human. The last place they were spotted was at the Halloween party at the manor. Her friends left her talking to a handsome guy and said they'd meet up with her later at the Laughing Hamster, and she never showed up. They gave it twenty-four hours in case she was having a wild fling, but she still hasn't turned up, and it's been a week."

"Fuck!" The expletive flies out of my mouth before I can stop it. This is such bad timing with the counsel keeping a close eye on the coven and their ability to run the portal. Not to mention nothing good can happen to a human if they run into supernatural trouble. "Do you have any leads?"

He shakes his head. "No. I came here as soon as I got the information. I'm heading out to the manor now to sniff around. They gave me one of her shirts so I have her scent. I was wondering if you'd want to assist. Two supernatural noses are better than one, and witches just don't have the same senses as us, so Regan won't be any help." He holds up a piece of material that I'm assuming belongs to the missing girl. A waft of sickly sweet perfume drifts in my direction, and I wrinkle my nose. Well, that smell's not going to be hard to miss.

I stand up, and he quickly follows suit. "The ground's fairly frozen now, so I'm not sure how much scent will remain, but he may have some security footage that shows where she went. The manor is fairly well covered for that. Just give me a moment to get changed," I tell him before using my vamp speed to run upstairs to my apartment above my office.

Shucking the suit I'd put on to look professional for Mr. Lee, I opt for jeans and a T-shirt. I also swap out my dress shoes for a pair of boots to protect my feet from the snow on the ground. After grabbing a jacket, I return to the foyer. Taylor's hair ruffles as the rush of wind from my movement brushes over him, and he startles, blinking his unusual green and orange eyes.

"Don't do that. It makes my tiger nervous, and I get

the urge to maul you," he rumbles, a ripple of energy washing over him as his tiger tries to force a shift.

I chuckle and gesture for him to lead the way. "Why don't we run out to the manor? You can shift and get out all that pent-up aggression," I tease, and he growls at me. I can tell his tiger is actually at the surface, so this missing human must really be throwing him off, because Taylor's control over his tiger is impeccable.

"Okay, but I'm going to strip in here if you don't mind. The older generation of coven women are pervs, and they always whistle and hoot if I have to change in public." His cheeks tinge red, his embarrassment obvious, and I chuckle.

"They really are bad, but they don't mean any harm. It's only when they've been indulging that they really make a fuss. Just take it as a compliment, and remember, the more they know it embarrasses you, the more they'll do it. I swear they are bored. Hopefully with their daughters returning to town, it will take all of their focus away from us single men. I'm sick of being told I should find a pretty witch and settle down, and then basically being given a portfolio of every woman in the coven. That's one of the reasons I left the damn vampire realm."

Taylor chuckles as he starts to strip, undoing the buttons on his khaki sheriff's shirt. "At least you've only had two years of it. I grew up here, and those women have repeatedly tried to set me up time and time again. It's why the children of the coven and the few others of us who grew up here vowed not to have any romantic entanglements with each other. The mothers' gloating would have been unbearable." He folds the shirt nicely before removing his pants until he's standing in just his underwear. "I guess that vow has gone out the window now. We knew it was just a matter of time with Ruby and Maddock. They've been dancing around each other since middle school. I can't say Tatiana and Reagan were much of a surprise either. I'm glad, because he deserves it. Susan did a real number on him."

A voice from the doorway has us both turning in surprise. "Well, I must say getting your seal of approval on my relationship status is a blessing, but hearing it while you're naked is just the icing on the cupcake." Ruby Miller is standing there with a big grin on her face, eyeing Taylor like he's a piece of meat.

"I'm not sure it's just the older generation of coven women you need to be worried about," I tell him out of the side of my mouth, and he scoffs.

"I already know Ruby is a perv. I can practically feel her eyes on my ass when I walk away." Taylor bends down and picks up his shoes, socks, and pants, adding them to the neat pile before he turns to the woman standing next to Ruby who looks a little shellshocked.

"Haven't you missed being home?" he asks, grinning at her and opening his arms wide. "Shall we hug it out?"

She puts her own hands out in a universal stop sign as Taylor goes to step closer.

"Eww, no, Taylor Crimson. I don't know where that body has been lately, and if I remember correctly, you haven't been too picky in the past." Her petite nose is screwed up, but her dark brown eyes are alight with laughter, and when she drops the fake scowl and smiles, I almost fall over with surprise. She's stunning.

Her eyes aren't just brown, but they have a hint of red in them, and her smile transforms her face into a thing of beauty. She has sharp cheekbones with a slightly pointy chin, and a cute button nose with a smattering of freckles. Her sleek, long black hair is pulled back into a ponytail at the base of her neck, and her lithe, toned body with just a hint of curves is encased nicely in her jeans and T-shirt. My heart skips a beat at the thought of stripping those casual clothes off of her and draping her in the finest silk sheets that just happen to be on my bed.

"Lucas. Lucas!" The sharp tone has me blinking and frowning at my friend.

"What?" I snarl, and he just grins, still standing in only his boxers, not ashamed of his body at all.

"I was just telling the girls that we're headed out to the manor to take a look around."

"The girls?" I raise a very unsubtle eyebrow, and while Taylor is clueless, Ruby is a lot better at social niceties. I bet Pru drilled that into her from a young age. Although she looks concerned about why we need to go out to the manor, she takes a moment to introduce the new woman to me.

"Mayor Sharpe," she starts, and I hold up a hand.

"How many times do I have to tell you it's Lucas, please."

She nods, smiling. "I have brought you the answer to all your troubles." She waves at the girl next to her like a game show host presenting a prize to a lucky winner, and I want to know what game I have to play to be that winner.

"And that is?" I ask, still slightly confused, and she drops her arms and stomps her foot just as her friend shuffles self-consciously.

"Allow me to introduce you to Tia Blackwood. Mr. Lee's granddaughter and master pyrotechnic artist. Tia, this is Lucas Sharpe, our mayor."

It's like angels sing out in chorus when I realize I really am the prize winner and this woman is the answer to my prayers.

"Please tell me you'll help." I clasp my hands together in prayer and get down on my knees. "If I have to go beg your grandfather one more time, I'd rather have a monster hunter just take my fangs and stake me."

I know I'm being silly, and from the look on Taylor's and Ruby's faces, neither of them knew I had it in me, but I need this woman, and the fact that she's beautiful and calls to me in a way I've never felt before is just the icing on the cake. I only hope I can have it and eat it too —in every single possible way.

She drops her arms and loses the frown, a small giggle escaping her mouth before she can stop it. I smile back, knowing I've got her but waiting to hear it from her lips.

"Yes, that's why I'm here. Ruby said you and the coven were in a bind, and all I want to do is help the people who were my family growing up."

I hear the tone and know there is more to the story than she is letting on, and judging by my own interaction with her grandfather, I'm not surprised. I climb to my feet and brush off my jeans.

"Thank you. You have no idea what this means to me. Shall we arrange to meet maybe tomorrow once you've settled in? I can tell you what we have planned."

She agrees, and Ruby slaps her hands together. "Right then, we will leave the two of you to whatever this was." She waves her hands between me and the mostly naked shifter. We both get what she is implying and start to argue, but she just giggles and turns, dragging Tia with her. "Bye, boys, and have fun."

We follow them out and watch them climb into an old Mustang convertible. Ruby starts it up, and the damn thing backfires, billowing smoke at us as they drive in the direction of the manor.

Taylor and I cough and splutter and wave the noxious fumes away. "She could fix that with magic but doesn't because she likes being a menace," he growls as he drops his underwear and shifts. His huge, orange and black tiger chuffs at me and brushes back and forth against my jeans before padding down the couple of stairs and nodding at his underwear.

"Yeah right, buddy. I am not picking those up. I'll grab the rest of the clothes though. You should have added them to the pile if you didn't want to go commando."

He huffs and stretches before taking off in the same direction as the convertible. I pop back into the office and grab his clothes, shoes, and hat before following after him.

CHAPTER
Three

Tia

Ruby heads in the direction of the manor. The top of her convertible is up, since it's too cold to have it down now, but the fit isn't great, and it's not long before my teeth start to chatter.

Ruby chuckles. "LA has made you soft, T," she tells me, and I shrug.

"I was recently diagnosed with an iron deficiency. My blood moves sluggishly around my body, and I suffer quite badly from the cold. I didn't think to pack extra warm things. It seems a lot colder here than it was in Toronto. Maybe it's because I was busy all the time."

"Really? Maybe you need to pop into Happy Herbs while you're here and chat with Minerva about what you might be able to do to help that. Meadow is home too, and I'm sure she would love to see you. Shit, maybe there is some kind of spell that can fix it."

Ruby seems so upbeat and positive, but as I watch

the scenery go by, all I feel is dread. This road is one I've hated traveling on all my life—not because of the manor, since Ruby's family has always been loving and kind, but because past the manor is my family home. It's a place where I have always felt like an outsider.

The Blackwood family farm is on a few acres in a secluded area, which is located about ten miles past the manor . It was the perfect place for my grandfather to set up his fireworks workshop when he first moved to the island and met my grandmother. She died before I was born, leaving just the three of us out there. He didn't attend coven meetings very often, preferring to stay secluded and focused on his work. He used to ship his specialty fireworks to covens all over the world for special ceremonies and celebrations. He didn't deal with humans very often, but enough to be known and respected for his skill in the community, even if they thought he was an asshole. Thankfully, because of his asshole ways, I got a lot of sympathy when I turned up on doorsteps, begging to be taught. He will never know how much he helped me. Everyone I learned from loved that they were getting one over on the grumpy, rude old asshole—their words, not mine.

My mother was a very active member of the coven as a teenager and into early adulthood, according to Pru. It was only after she got pregnant with me that she started to become withdrawn and noncommunicative.

Growing up in a house with a mother who barely even looked at me and a grandfather who was actively hostile was not a fun place to live. I used to beg my mother to leave, to take up a room at the manor offered by Pru until we could get back onto our feet, but she would just look at me blankly and tell me not to be so ridiculous.

Eventually she stopped attending coven gatherings altogether, and nothing her friends said could change her mind. I also begged her to tell me where my father was and which coven he was from so I could get to know him, but all she and my grandfather would tell me was that he was a drifter who hadn't even stuck around after he discovered Mom was pregnant. My grandfather was particularly antagonistic toward the man. My mother just seemed sad every time I mentioned him, so I eventually stopped asking.

My grandfather has been actively hostile toward me for as long as I can remember. I would often compare myself to Cinderella. I was expected to do all the cooking and cleaning because my mother seemed to exist in a fugue state at home. It was only when we would go into town that she would show any signs of life, but Grandfather was never far from her, and I guess asking her friends for help would have meant trouble once we went back home.

I worked for Pru at Candy Conniptions all through high school and had saved every penny. The only reason I was allowed to work there was because she bulldozed my grandfather, and she is so damn power-ful, not even he could say no to her. The minute I had my diploma in hand, I was on the first ferry away from Morbank Island.

I will help the town out for this one occasion, and then I will leave once more and never return.

"Do you know what kind of show Mayor Sharpe wants for this Feast and Fireworks thing?" I ask my friend as I feel my body growing more tense. We're not even going to my family's place, I'm going to be staying at the manor, but I'm like Pavlov's dog, and my response is automatic.

I need something to distract me, and thinking about the mayor and his current project is a good option, especially when the good mayor turned out to be a smoking hot vampire who oozes danger and sex appeal. I was expecting a much older sedate man, so to say I was surprised is an understatement. Mayor Sharpe is sexy in a jeans and T-shirt, so he must be devastating in a suit. His dark blond hair is thick and luscious, and my fingers itched to run through it. When he smiled, I saw a brief flash of fangs and was instantly intrigued. We've never had a lot of vampires on Morbank, and he is certainly one fine specimen of the species. Vampires age differently, so although he looks to be in his late twenties, he could be hundreds of years old. I'm insanely attracted to him, but I'm pretty sure I hid it well. I've become very adept at keeping my emotions buried deep down.

Ruby turns at the gates to the manor, and I find my gaze drifting farther up the road. She must notice. "Did you want to go see your mother?" she asks quietly, and I quickly shake my head.

"No. I have nothing to say to that woman, although I probably need to face my grandfather at some point. I wouldn't put it past him to try to sabotage anything I do."

"Are you going to be able to make the rockets here? Or will you have to return to LA to do that?" Ruby navigates the lane to the manor with the ease of having done it all her life.

I scoff. "There is no way Grandfather will let me within ten feet of his precious warehouse. I will either have to return to LA or ask them to ship what I need and then make the modifications when they get here."

"Modifications?" Ruby sounds intrigued as she parks the car in front of the manor. A young man runs out and nods to her, holding out his hand, but she shakes her head as she gets out.

"That's okay, Jessie, just leave it there. I'm not going to be long, and I wouldn't want you to have to try to start it."

The look of relief on the boy's face is comical. He's obviously driven Ruby's "classic" piece of junk before.

"Okay, thanks, Ruby," he replies before returning to wherever he came from.

"Who was that?" I ask, pointing at his retreating form.

"Oh, that's Jesse. He works as a valet here now," Ruby says, going around and grabbing my case out of the trunk before slamming it closed. "Come on. And what modifications are you talking about? Your grandpa's rockets were always amazing. I'm assuming he was able to create scenes in the sky using magic, right?"

"Yes." I let her carry my case. There's no point in arguing with her once she has her mind set on something. "That was something I had to work out on my own through trial and error, and to be honest, even though I know how to in theory, my magic is so weak I've never been able to get it to work, which is why I've stuck to human fireworks. I'm a little worried that I'm going to let the mayor down because my magic has always been lackluster at best."

Just as I finish speaking, a whoosh of displaced air blows our hair around, and the aforementioned mayor appears before us, holding a bundle of clothes.

Ruby screeches and hurls my case at him. He drops the pile of clothes in shock and puts his hands up to protect himself from the heavy object hurtling at his body. Ruby's eyes widen, and she thrusts out her hands, stopping the case midair. It hovers there as both she and the mayor breathe out a sigh of relief.

The snort of laughter bubbles out of my nose before I can help it, and they both turn to look at me. I clamp my lips shut, but it's no good. That was the funniest thing I've seen in ages, and I let the laughter tumble out. The two of them are very patient with me while I lose my shit. It feels so good to laugh, and I just let it all out. Ruby taps her foot in annoyance, but Mayor Sharpe is indulgent, and there's an amused gleam in his eyes, and the corners of his lips tip up too.

"Oh my god, Ruby, that was so funny." My laughter dies off into little giggles, and my friend rolls her eyes.

"Damn vampire speed, freaks me out every time. I'm just not used to it." She smooths her hands over her jeans as the door to the manor bangs open and her brother, Regan, appears at the top of the steps.

"What's wrong? Is everything okay?" he demands, looking around, his muscles coiled and ready for anything.

"Sorry, Regan, I scared Ruby when I appeared out of nowhere," Mayor Sharpe says, and Regan's worry clears from his face before his gaze meets mine.

"Tia Blackwell, as I live and breathe. So you weren't able to say no to my very insistent sister either, were you? Tatiana was also able to drag Meadow back to us as well. We now have almost half of you back on the island." Regan sounds pleased, and his eyes crease slightly when he smiles.

Shit, I blinked and we all grew up. I feel a slight pang of sadness that I missed it.

"Yes!" Ruby fist pumps the air, and we laugh at her antics, but I soon have to put a damper on my amusement. I don't want anyone to think I'm here to stay.

"I'm here to help Mayor Sharpe, and then I'm leaving again. There's nothing here on the island for me." Everyone sobers up quickly at that, and there's an uncomfortable silence.

"Well I, for one, am grateful that you agreed to come back, even if it is temporary," Mayor Sharpe says with a grateful smile. "I was beginning to think I wasn't going to be able to fulfill my end of the agreement and provide fireworks with our feast." I look at the man with twinkling gray eyes, and when he smiles, there's another slight flash of fang, and I feel something twinge down low. I'm thankful that he took the initiative to break the loaded silence.

"Well, I know why the two of you are here, and I have Tia's room ready for her, but why are you here, Lucas?" Regan's brow wrinkles in confusion just as a large, orange and black white tiger comes loping up the driveway. "Oh, and the sheriff. This must be something serious. You better all come in, and I'll get us drinks. Whatever it is, I'd like to get it taken care of before our first busload of realm tourists arrives next week, and tell

Taylor to cover his ass before he comes into my manor, there are children here." Regan turns and hurries back inside.

The three of us watch as Taylor slows, his tongue hanging out of his mouth as he tries to catch his breath. Before he can shift, though, a hurricane consisting of two small, red-haired children comes flying out of the manor door.

"Tiger Taylor, you've come to play!" one of the voices shouts as the two kids throw their arms around the tiger.

Taylor huffs and collapses onto his belly, and the children giggle as they climb all over him. He is gentle as the three of them roll around and wrestle on the ground, and we watch on in amusement.

"Who are they?" I ask, even though I have a feeling I know exactly who they are.

"They are Regan's twins, Kady and Kadir, and they are a terrible twosome. They are also about to get eaten by a tiger if they are not careful," Ruby says with a raised voice, and the children stop what they are doing with the tiger and look up at the sound of her voice.

"Taylor won't eat us, Aunt Wuby. He woves us," the little boy says, shaking his head, but the little girl's eyes drift to me.

"Oh, someone new." She scrambles to her feet and hurries over before stopping directly in front of me. "Hi, I'm Kady Miller. Who are you?" She holds out her hand and patiently waits for me to respond.

"Hi, I'm Tia Blackwell," I reply, taking her hand, charmed by her manners.

"Who are you and what have you done with my

niece?" Ruby looks around, peering into a bush on the side of the path and even going so far as to shove Taylor over so she can look underneath him. The twins giggle, and Kady shakes her head.

"Don't be silly, Aunt Ruby. Tati says it's polite to greet people with a handshake."

"Holy shit, will wonders never cease?" Ruby stops her silliness and stares at her niece in amazement. "Who would have thought that Tatiana would be a good influence?" she jokes, and Kady giggles.

"That's a dollar in the swear jar, Aunt Wuby," the boy calls. He still has his arms wrapped around Taylor's neck. Taylor stands up, and Kadir whoops with excitement. That's when Mayor Sharpe steps forward, and both of the twins fall silent and stare at him. Kady grips my hand harder and shuffles in next to me. I guess they hadn't noticed him until now, and I'm not surprised, because he's good at being still.

"If you don't mind, Kadir, Taylor needs to shift, and then we need to speak with your father. Would it be alright if you continued this at another time?"

Kadir's eyes bulge, and he sits up on Taylor's back before sliding off and hurrying over to Mayor Sharpe. He stares up at him, but he's obviously not satisfied because he tugs at his shirt until Lucas gets down to his level.

"Can I touch one of your fangs?" Kadir whispers, and Ruby gasps in shock.

"Kadir, no. I'm sorry, Lucas. The kids have never met a vampire, and they've been asking a lot of questions recently. I think they overheard a few things about their father and Tatiana's trip into the vampire realm.

Their ears flap like an elephant's, and we have to be careful what we talk about around them."

Lucas chuckles, and it's like a light shines above him, illuminating the hotness of the man. "You can't touch them because they are very sharp and will cut you, but you can see them." He smiles widely, and I watch as his fangs lengthen until they are prominent in his mouth.

"Whoa!" Kadir exclaims and leans in to get a closer look.

Lucas doesn't even flinch, and Kady lets go of my hand and cautiously steps over. Phew, gorgeous and kind to children, that's certainly a winning combination. I don't have time for romantic entanglements, though, and certainly not with a man who has made his home in a place I detest.

"And you drink blood?" Kadir asks, his eyes wide. Kady grabs his hand and steps up next to him, not wanting to be left out but not as brave as Kadir.

"I do. It's essential to vampires, just like air is essential to breathe."

"Do you eat other things?" Kady whispers, and Lucas winks at her.

"We sure do, and your Aunt Ruby's treats are some of my favorite things, so I have to make sure that I clean my fangs as well as you brush your teeth. I don't want to get holes in them, that would hurt."

Oh shit, this man is killing me. Maybe I do need to take a trip out to the Blackwell farm to reaffirm my decision not to stay. I could easily find myself changing my mind if I spend too much time here.

"Okay, you two, that's enough. Both Mayor Sharpe

and Sheriff Taylor have been more than patient, but Taylor needs to change into his human form, and we need to speak to Daddy about a few things. Why don't you run off and see if you can find Sugar for me. It's almost her dinner time, and you guys can be in charge of feeding her," Ruby suggests.

"Oh, I want to see Taylor change though," Kadir argues, losing interest in Lucas, who stands back up.

"Oh yes, me too," Kady chimes in, and Ruby huffs in exasperation.

"No, he will be naked when he changes, and nobody needs to see that. Run along."

Kady wrinkles her nose at learning he's going to be naked, but Kadir's eyes just widen further.

"That's awesome. I wish I was a shifter too."

Ruby rolls her eyes and grabs the twins by the hand and drags them back into the manor. "I'm sure you'll run around naked plenty when you're older, so let's save it for then, shall we?" she says as the door closes behind them.

"Alright, let's leave him to it. Sorry about dropping your clothes on the ground, but Ruby tried to kill me with a suitcase," Lucas apologizes to Taylor. Taylor chuffs and rolls his tiger eyes.

Lucas doesn't seem too concerned about his friend's annoyance. He just grabs the still hovering suitcase out of the air and puts his hand on my back. "Shall we, or do you want to see him naked too?"

The last part of that question is asked with a growly voice that makes a shiver travel down my back. I just shake my head, unable to form words, and Lucas looks pleased.

"Well, good. Don't be long, Taylor." He guides me into the manor.

I thought he'd be cool since he's a vampire, but his hand is like fire through my T-shirt, and I can only think about what the rest of him would feel like pressed up against me, naked.

Lucas sniffs the air and stumbles slightly before righting himself, but the look he gives me is pure fire, and I have a feeling he knows exactly what I'm thinking. I can't decide if I want to run and have the predator I can see just below the surface chase me down or run as fast and as far as I can, screw the fireworks.

CHAPTER
Four

Lucas

The scent of Tia's arousal is mouthwatering, and I can't get my fangs to retract after dropping them down for Kadir and Kady. The kids are cute, and they provided a good momentary distraction from my worry about the missing human and my attraction to the beautiful woman watching everything with interest. Tia Blackwell is a conundrum. I am incredibly attracted to her, but I have a feeling she's trying her hardest to keep everyone at arm's length. She was also straightforward about reminding everyone that her visit to the island was a temporary arrange- ment and that she can't wait to see it in her rearview mirror again.

There must be more to the story of her childhood than I know. With my few short interactions with Mr. Lee, it doesn't really surprise me that she doesn't want to be here. He is a vile man, and I haven't said that about anyone else on this island. Everyone from the coven and supernatural community has been incredibly welcoming, and even the human residents have been cordial if somewhat wary, but that's to be expected. Their knowledge of vampires is from movies and literature, and we aren't always portrayed in a positive light, not to mention there are always good and bad in all races.

I will tread carefully, because I don't want her to turn tail and run before I get what I want from her both professionally and personally. Her scent calls to the predator inside me, and it makes me want to whisk her away to my apartment and not let her up until I've tasted every part of her.

The foyer of the manor is empty apart from a woman behind the desk. Julie waves at me enthusiastically. The woman is one of the nonlocals who works for the town due to the decline in locals, which we now know is due to a spell that's designed to chase them away. Her twin sister works over at the candy store for Ruby. Neither of them has been particularly welcoming to the returning coven women, and Taylor just recently discovered that they are supes from another witch coven. The Wives of the Rowan Tree are a rival coven who claimed to be the rightful caretakers of the portal. There was a battle between them and the Arbor Vitae Coven hundreds of years ago for the right to the island, and the only reason that finished was because the goddess stepped in and named the Arbor Vitae Coven as the true guardians, putting a stop to the war. The rival coven slinked off in defeat, but of course, in the atypical clichéd manner, they promised revenge. Up until now, they haven't attempted anything, but why are they here, working for Arbor Vitae businesses, if they are not here to start something? We are keeping an eye on them, which is easier when they are working for us.

"Oh, Mayor Sharpe, it is lovely to see you today. What brings you out to the manor?"

She flat-out ignores the woman next to me as we approach the desk, and before I can answer, I hear a throat clear behind me.

"Official business, I'm afraid, Julie. If you'll excuse us, we're meeting Regan in the lounge." Taylor is a little gruff, and Julie looks surprised, but now that all the local supes know about the spell on the island, they are wary of the newcomers, especially ones who have benefited from the girls being gone. Taylor had a little thing with their friend Mia, but I think he backed away out of respect for his long-term friends. Taylor grew up with the coven kids, and if Ruby and Tatiana say there's something not quite right with that group of girls, then he's going to listen to them.

"Well, did you want to leave your friend to check in with me?" she asks, raising a questioning eyebrow at Tia.

"No, that will be fine, thanks, Julie." Ruby steps out of the lift and holds the door open. "Come on, Regan and Tatiana are waiting. The kids are distracted, and we can show Tia to her room once we are done."

Without looking back, I guide Tia to the lift with Taylor trailing closely behind, but when we step in, I catch Julie frowning at us and picking up a phone to make a phone call. The doors to the elevator close before she speaks, and although my hearing is good, I can't catch what she says as the elevator moves upwards, putting a floor between us.

Regan is standing behind the bar in their cocktail lounge when we arrive, with Tatiana sitting at one of the bar stools. The elevator doors close behind us, and Ruby waves an arm, placing a blocking spell so no one can hear what we are talking about.

"Hey, guys." Tatiana waves at us before squealing and jumping off her seat and throwing her arms around Tia. "Oh my goodness, it is so good to see you."

As the girls exchange hugs and quiet words, we give them a little privacy, and Regan offers Taylor and me a beer. I place Tia's suitcase out of the way before joining them at the bar.

"Nah, I probably shouldn't, I have to do some investigating." Taylor wrinkles his nose. "Maybe after we're done."

Regan frowns but nods. "And you?" he asks, and I shake my head as well.

"No, I'm here to help Taylor, so I'll abstain for now as well."

"Well, now I'm really worried. I thought this might have been about the Thanksgiving party, but I'm assuming it's not."

"No, unfortunately, it's something worse," Taylor replies as the girls turn their attention back to us. Tia and Tatiana are a little glassy-eyed, but they seem ready to listen.

"Hang on. Before we do this, I need to give Tia

something to drink." Tatiana waves her hand, and a golden flask appears on the bar top in front of her seat.

"Ah, no, I already gave it to her back in Canada," Ruby argues, frowning at Tatiana.

Tatiana narrows her eyes and looks carefully at Tia. "But she still has a spell on her, can't you see it?"

Ruby turns and looks at the woman in question, who squirms slightly before crossing her arms defensively and raising an eyebrow at her two friends.

"What are you two doing?" she asks, and Ruby waves an absent hand at her.

"Hush," she hisses.

"Oh shit," Taylor says and steps back, grabbing my arm and pulling me with him.

"Ruby Miller, you did not just tell me to hush, did you?" Tia demands and starts to spark. It looks like tiny little fireworks are bursting off her body. It's so pretty, I reach out to touch it, but Taylor slaps my hand down.

On his side of the bar, Regan has moved farther away from the girls. "Tia claims to have no power, but her body always sparks like that when she's emotional. When she tries to use it, though, it always fizzles out," he explains as the three of us watch.

"Oh my god, you're right. It is still there. How?" Ruby looks at Tatiana, who shrugs.

"I have no idea. Master Alsorin said the two potions would break the geas and fix our magic waste."

"What if the spell on Tatiana is something old, far older than the two other spells?" Regan's eyebrows are furrowed together in a frown as he steps around the bar and moves closer to the other two witches. His eyes narrow in concentration as he stares at Tia. "It may explain why she never had the kind of power she should have. See the dark shadow that sort of hugs her body? It's like an aura but not. I can only see it now that we are really looking for it."

Tia's golden skin pales considerably, and she wobbles, grabbing hold of the bar to steady herself. It's all I can do to stop myself from jumping forward and wrapping my arms around her. What is happening to me? I'm reacting like a vampire would react to his mate. Could she be?

"Grandfather," Tia whispers quietly, her eyes widening in realization. "Once a year, he would perform a spell. He claimed it was to help me with what pathetic little bit of magic I had, and I always went along with it with the feeble hope that it might work one day, but what if it was the opposite? There was one he would perform for my mother too. It was a spell to bring my father back, but that never worked either. I just assumed it was because he was a crappy witch, but then his fireworks are incredible, so I couldn't understand why he couldn't perform other spells."

"That bastard," Ruby spits. "We need to go see him right now," she announces, turning and heading for the elevator.

"Hold up." Taylor jumps forward, stopping Ruby in her tracks. "If Mr. Lee is performing spells on his family without their knowledge, he will need to be dealt with by the coven. He has broken coven law, but if you wait, I will accompany you out to the Blackwood farm to give you some official support."

Ruby starts to argue, but I stop her.

"Taylor is right. I have no doubt you two are

powerful enough to defend yourselves, but if Mr. Lee has been doing this for years, then he must have prepared for it to be discovered. Having both Taylor and I there for backup would be wise, but this issue is also extremely important."

"What *is* this issue?" Reagan demands, sounding frustrated.

"A human has gone missing, and she was last seen at the manor, attending the haunted house last week. She left with a stranger and never returned," Taylor explains, and Regan blows out a huge sigh, dropping his head.

"Fuck," he mutters succinctly. "That means my realm tours will be in jeopardy. I have a group arriving in two days. Are we sure she isn't just shacked up with someone and forgot to inform her family?"

Taylor shakes his head. "No, her friends were adamant that she's missing. They have some kind of system for booty calls. I was hoping we could get a look at your security footage, and Lucas and I could have a sniff around." He taps the side of his nose, and Regan agrees.

"Yes please. The sooner we figure this out, the better. Although the island's tourism has increased, the realm tours were going to guarantee there was never going to be a shortage of visitors to the island. They can't be canceled before they've even started. Come on, the security room is on the same level as the portal, so I'll have to swipe us all down there. Are you all coming?" he asks the girls who have been huddled around Tia for support while they listened.

Ruby shakes her head. "No, we'll wait here. I'd like

to fill Mom in on what we've found. I'd like her to come out to the Blackwell farm with us."

Taylor shudders. "If anyone can scare old Mr. Lee straight, it will be Pru. That woman is formidable, and I do not want to be on her bad side."

He's not wrong. Not much scares me, but the sheer power that sparks off that woman is incredible. Her whole family is super powerful, and I can imagine in another twenty years or so, Ruby will feel that way too. The men are not as strong as the women, but Regan will still be a force to be reckoned with. Being in the same room with Pru makes my fangs itch.

We move to the elevator, but Tatiana stops us, wringing her hands with worry. "This might be nothing, but I swear I felt the portal open the night of the Halloween celebrations, and earlier too when I had first arrived back. I was out trying to grow the cornfield, and I felt this weird magical residue. It was only after we had gone through the portal ourselves that I realized what it was. I didn't think much of it, but now that a girl is missing, well, I guess it feels significant."

"But I was under the impression the portal can only be accessed and operated by a coven member," I say, and Regan scowls.

"And you would be right, which means we have a traitor if the portal is being operated at times outside of the schedule."

"Both times were in the evening, and I know it stops running at a certain time," Tatiana explains. "But I had so much on my mind, what with us traveling into the realms and the haunted house and the fake Regans and then Marco, I forgot about it until now. I'm so sorry."

"I probably would have forgotten too," Ruby assures her friend. "And yes, it's not supposed to run after nine."

"Alright, so I need to check the operational log for those two days too. I can't believe I haven't felt it myself." Regan shoves a frustrated hand through his red hair, leaving it sticking out at all angles.

"Don't be so hard on yourself, man. You've been up to your eyeballs in trying to keep this place afloat, as well as being a father to the twins, so I'm shocked you're even standing by the end of the day. It's no surprise that you didn't feel the residual magic, especially if it's happening late at night." Taylor tries to assure his friend, but Regan doesn't look convinced.

"Come on then, let's get to the bottom of this so we can help Tia with her problems." My fingers itch to reach out to the woman who looks lost and sad. She's been following the conversation, but she seems to be lost in her head as well. Finding out there's some kind of spell on you and that your family member may be responsible is not fun.

I know all about unfun family politics. My father was the vampire ambassador to the fae realm for many years, and he wanted me to follow in his footsteps. That was not my idea of fun at all, and I refused to. Instead, my sister Antoinette took the position, eager to leave the vampire realm so she didn't have to watch the men she was so attracted to whore their way around the palace.

Jacob, Jett, and Jeremiah, along with their cousin Cole, were my best friends growing up, and Nettie was the annoying kid sister we all tolerated. There was great pressure on them growing up due to their father being king of the vampires. They took any chance they got to escape the pressure of impending rule and dragged the rest of us along. We got into mischief as often as we could, and both Cole and I could see the crush my sister harbored for the triplets, but nothing became of it because they saw her as a little sister, much to her disappointment.

Twenty-five years ago, tragedy struck, and the king disappeared, never to be seen again. The triplets' mother was only a consort, so she could not rule in his stead, and the task fell to them centuries earlier than they had anticipated. For years, Antoinette suffered in silence as women paraded themselves around for the triplets, eager to be chosen as their mates, but they were happy to sample the wares without promising anything. I watched with anger and annoyance as Antoinette shrank into a shell of her former self, despondent and listless, until I couldn't take it any longer. When Dad announced his retirement, I insisted she take his position. She gratefully accepted and escaped to the fae realm so she no longer had to see them, and although my father doesn't speak to me now, it was worth it. With my father refusing to talk to me, and my sister residing in the fae realm, there was nothing keeping me at home. I was so angry with my friends that I also decided to leave, and that's how I ended up as the mayor of Morbank Island two years ago. I haven't regretted the decision one bit, but I do miss my mother.

"Yeah, I wish I could say I can't believe Mr. Lee would do such a thing, but I can't. The man is horrible, and finding out that he has spelled Tia and Fiona for all these years doesn't surprise me in the least. I just hope we can break whatever spell he has on them," Regan says as the elevator comes to a stop, and we step into it, allowing it to take us down to the portal room.

CHAPTER
Five

Lucas

I haven't been down here since I first arrived in the human realm. No one is in the waiting room, since regular realm jumps are only being done twice a week, but that will change to daily jumps after the first scheduled realm tour.

Regan leads us to the operating room. Mac, one of the four coven members who is in charge of operating the portal, looks up, his eyebrows jumping in surprise when he sees us.

"Sheriff, Mayor Sharpe, good to see you." Mac nods to both of us respectively. He's of Pru's generation of coven members and a great guy. He plays Santa every Christmas for the kids in the town. Obviously, the real Santa is too busy at Christmas to take time to stop in at the island, but Mac's a good substitute, and the kids love him.

"Hey, Mac." Taylor nods.

"Good to see you, Mac," I say, but his brow creases as Regan walks over to a bank of screens opposite the portal console.

He spins his chair. "What's going on?"

Regan tells him about the missing girl and explains that the haunted house was the last place she was seen. "I'm going to pull up the security footage around the manor and see if we can't see where she went."

Mac purses his lips. "Shit, that's the last thing we need. Hopefully she left with someone, and she's just being a bad friend."

Taylor shoves his hand into his pocket and pulls out his phone. He swipes his finger a couple of times, brings up a photo, and hands it to me before giving it to Regan. "This is Olivia, the girl who went missing. Her friends said that when they last saw her, she was heading from the cornfield maze to the haunted house with the guy she had been flirting with all night. They were going to go through the manor's haunted house and then all meet back at the Laughing Hamster for drinks later. They thought she'd be fine, even though she'd only just met the man earlier in the day, because they were surrounded by lots of people here for the Halloween celebration."

"Okay, if I pull up all the security footage for that night, I can use a spell to zero in on her face—kind of like witchy facial recognition," Regan says as he runs his fingers over the keyboard.

Taylor's eyebrows jump in surprise. "Really? Wow, that's seriously handy."

Regan grimaces. "Yeah, I discovered it when the kids decided that hiding from me during hide-and-seek and not coming out when I called 'game over' was fun. I've had to use it to locate them numerous times within the manor."

Taylor and I chuckle at the twins' antics, and although he sounds frustrated, I can see affection and pride glowing in his eyes when he talks about his kids. I want that someday. I was always hoping to have a mate to share it with.

"Okay, here she is." He points to a few screens that show views of the corn maze.

"You had cameras in the maze?" I ask, unable to hide my surprise, and he grins.

"Magic is a wonderful thing. I thought it was better to be safe than sorry, and we had someone watching the whole time in case kids got lost and upset. We were able to send in a guide to show them the way out." He points at another screen, which shows a crying six-year-old child. Suddenly, a tiny, friendly-looking witch on a broom appears in front of the child and I hear it say, "Follow me," in an enthusiastic high-pitched voice. We watch as it leads the child out of the maze and directly to its frantic parents who shout with relief and gather him up in their arms.

"That's so cool. Can we organize something like that for the Feast and Fireworks in case we get any lost children?" I ask him, suitably impressed with the coven's ingenuity.

"Of course. I had some set up in the orchard too." The same girl appears on camera in the back of the cart being pulled by the tractor through the orchard. We watch as the guy she's with leans in and starts kissing her, his hands wandering up her top.

"Is it just me or is that guy's face slightly blurry?" Taylor asks, leaning in, and I freeze, using my enhanced eyesight to get a better look. It's almost like looking through binoculars, and I can zoom in.

"That's a fucking vampire, and he is obscuring his face by intermittently pulsing his skin so fast that it will blur his image for technology or from a distance, but look normal to the person he's with. It's a trick we've used for years, even before technology."

"A vampire? What would a vampire want with a human?" Regan asks, and I can't stop the snort of disgust that escapes my mouth.

"Well, blood, of course. Human blood is a delicacy for vampires and not something that is easily accessible. There have been occasional, pop-up black markets in the vampire realm, but the kings have been very quick to stamp them out."

"Can you do something to clear that up so we can see what's happening?" Taylor waves a hand at the screen, and Regan shrugs.

"I don't think so because it's something he's doing, not the cameras." It doesn't matter, though, because I watch in horror as the man leans in, and although his face is blurred, it is not hard to guess what he's doing when he nuzzles her neck and she throws her head back in ecstasy, her orgasm echoing through the speakers of the camera before he puts a hand over her mouth, silencing her.

"Holy shit, that is some venom you guys have." Mac sounds somewhat impressed, and I smother the smile that wants to creep across my face. Now is not the time.

"Without seeing his face, we have no way of

knowing if he is a vampire who has clearance to be on Earth or one who snuck in." Regan pushes away from the security screen as the camera continues to follow the couple on the rest of their hayride, but the vampire is smart and finishes his meal. He pulls away and makes her look him in the eye, obviously wiping her memory. He leaves her momentarily and does the same thing to the man driving the tractor, also wiping his memory of what happened before returning to his spot next to the girl.

Regan wheels his chair over next to Mac and presses a few buttons. "Why are you pulling up the log?" Mac frowns, watching Regan.

"Because Tatiana claims to have felt the portal operating on days when it wasn't supposed to be," Regan tells him.

"But that information is logged manually, so if someone did operate it, it would be easy enough to hide it."

"Well, yes and no. Although you are supposed to log all trips and who is going and where, every time the portal activates, there is a timestamp log, and that's something that happens automatically, and only my family has access to the records. It's just a little fail-safe, and one we have never needed to access before," Regan tells Mac when he looks a little disgruntled. "Here it is. The night Tatiana arrived home at ten thirty at night, and again on Halloween at a quarter to midnight."

"William was working on Halloween. I was scheduled, but I wanted to take my grandkids to the maze and hayride, so we swapped. He was more than happy to. He really likes the night shifts. I thought it was because he was a lazy asshole and almost no one ever travels at night, but what if it's for another reason?" Mac practically has steam shooting out of his ears by the end of his sentence.

Regan presses another couple of buttons. "And he was working the night Tatiana arrived home too."

We turn back to look at the security screens and watch the girl and the vamp get off the hayride. Regan hurriedly wheels his chair back to the monitors, and we observe as the camera angle changes, tracking them back to the manor house. They enter the manor, and the girl tugs the vamp toward the start of the haunted house, but he shakes his head and leads her to the elevator.

"What are they doing? The haunted house was on the ground floor," Taylor says as we watch them get into the elevator.

"Maybe he has a room and they are going back for sex. Feeding is a very sexual experience for a vampire, and he'll want to fuck," I tell them bluntly, and I see Taylor's eyes widen minutely before he gets his reaction under control.

Mac chuckles. "That was decidedly not very mayor-like, Lucas."

Instead of going up, however, the elevator lights show it going down. "Son of a bitch," Regan swears, pressing a few more buttons, and the camera switches to one that shows the portal waiting room. Sure enough, the doors open, and out walks the vampire, who's still obscured, but the girl now looks like she's been tranced. Her eyes are blank, and her movements are robotic as the portal flares to life, and we watch as they walk through together, the vampire waving to the person operating the portal.

"Fuck!" Taylor shouts, and I feel my stomach sink.

"Can you pull up the portal footage of the night Tatiana returned?" I ask Regan, who quickly complies. My stomach sinks even further as, once again, we watch the same thing happen, and an obscured vampire leads a tranced human—male this time—through the portal, and it closes behind them.

"How many times has the portal been operational when it wasn't supposed to be?" Taylor asks, unable to drag his eyes away from the footage repeating over and over again now that Regan has put it on a loop.

Regan gets up and hurries back to the console. The tension in the room is high as he mutters under his breath. "Holy hell. Fifty times in the last three months." His answer makes me feel sick, and I sink into a spare chair.

"What do you think they are doing with them?" Taylor looks at me, and I grimace with disgust.

"If I'm right, they are using them to start a blood farm. Human blood is a delicacy, so over the years, many have tried the same thing, but the kings have always stamped it out. I guess they are making another play at it. Fuck. With unfettered access to the portal, I guess they have been more successful than they have been in the past. They've never tried to bring the humans to the vamp realm before, just come over here and trafficked blood bags. They've really upped the stakes this time," I say, feeling ill.

It's a whole new level of evil. But how? And more importantly, who? The portal opens in the palace. How are they hiding that many humans from the residents of the palace? Surely one of the guards would notice, but if they are being paid off, then I'm certain they would turn a blind eye. It's getting them out of the palace that would be a challenge, because there are always people around.

"It looks like I'll be making a trip home." I sigh and stand up, brushing invisible dirt off my jeans, not wanting to look at anyone. "The kings will want to know about this immediately, and they will assign a team to find and return them."

"If they are alive," Mac points out dryly, and I nod.

"Yes, there's a possibility they aren't, but I doubt it. They would want to keep their cash cows healthy and alive and producing. Killing them is counterproductive. They may all need a mind wipe or some fake memories implanted so they aren't scarred for life, but they should be in fairly good condition," I explain. "Let's head back upstairs now that we don't need to sniff around and help Tia with her problem before I return to the vampire realm. I want to make sure everything is on track here for Feast and Fireworks before I leave. I'm not sure how long I'll be gone, and I don't want to leave things hanging."

"Great idea. Mac, we need to deal with William. I'll speak to my mother and see how she would like to handle it. I don't think I need to ask you to keep it to yourself. We don't want him to be tipped off."

"Of course. That bastard needs to pay. No punishment is enough for an asshole who allows people to be trafficked for whatever reason."

"The vampire kings may ask for his head," I warn

them, and the three men exchange a glance and Taylor shrugs.

"So be it. He's not stupid, and he's obviously doing it with malicious intentions."

"I'd like to know why, though, before we hand him over, but a truth potion is easy enough. I'm sure Mom will be happy to negotiate with the vampire kings."

Despite how angry I am, I chuckle when I think about the triplets having to face down Pru. I'm sure they'd rather desiccate than argue with the powerful woman. "I'd like to be in the room when it happens. I can't wait to see my old friends squirm."

We say goodbye to Mac. William isn't scheduled to work again for three more days, which gives us some time to put a plan into action. When we arrive upstairs, the girls are still in the lounge, but Laura Woods and Prudence Miller have joined them, and from the way Pru's hair is floating around her head, I can guess she's not in a good mood. She whirls on us as we step out of the elevator, and lightning flashes in her eyes.

"Are you finally done so we can go and deal with this… man!" She spits out the last bit like it's poison on her tongue.

Taylor and I step back, and Taylor shoves Regan forward.

"You tell her about the other thing." He's a smart man, our sheriff. I'm pretty sure if either of us told her the other bad news, we wouldn't be safe. Hopefully her son will be.

Pru looks between the three of us, and her hair lifts higher as her body starts to levitate off the floor. "What could be worse than a coven member spelling his own family without their consent?"

Regan holds up his hands. "Now, Mom, why don't you take a breath and center yourself? I really like the manor, and a stray lightning bolt inside could start a fire. Kady and Kadir are here somewhere, and you don't want them to be accidentally hurt, do you?"

Regan's words work, and Pru lowers back to the floor and her hair drops, curling itself into a bun and fastening at the base of her neck. The lightning in her eyes settles, only flickering with the occasional flash now and then. I guess that's as good as it's going to get.

Regan explains about the missing girl and what we've discovered. Although lightning crackles around her body, she manages to control it. I think Ruby grabbing hold of her arm may have siphoned off some of the excess rage, though, because Ruby closes her eyes and grits her teeth during the conversation, her own pink hair sticking out like she stuck her finger in a socket before dropping down again.

"This is a conspiracy. It has to be. A way to discredit the Arbor Vitae Coven and our running of the portal."

"Now, Pru, let's not jump to conclusions. It could easily just be a moneymaking scheme," Taylor says, taking his life into his own hands by playing devil's advocate.

Pru whirls on him and lifts a brow. "Really, Taylor? You think this is just a coincidence?" Taylor sighs, shaking his head.

"No, probably not, but we need all the facts. We can't pull the trigger until we know who to aim it at, so to speak," he replies calmly.

She waves her hand in the air, the movement jerky and agitated, but she nods. "Yes, you are right. One problem at a time. We will confront Mr. Lee." She grinds her teeth when she says the man's name. "And then Lucas will return to the vampire realm to get to the bottom of this. I, of course, will take over running Feasts and Fireworks so you do not have to worry," she tells me, and I smother the smile that wants to break out across my face and nod my thanks.

"That's much appreciated, Pru. I know it will be wonderful in your capable hands."

She preens slightly, and Taylor nudges me in the side. "Kiss ass," he whispers, and I shake my head.

"No, I'm just not stupid."

"Right, shall we go? If we head down to the lobby, we can teleport to Blackwell farm," Pru suggests, and Taylor shudders and shakes his head.

"Nope, I'll run. Teleporting does bad things to my tiger."

"And I can't teleport," Tia reminds them, and I can hear the disappointment in her voice.

"I'll carry you," I offer, stepping forward before I can even think about my response.

Ruby and Pru narrow their eyes on me in an almost identical way, and I swallow around the lump that just formed in my throat. Shit!

"Yes, that is a wonderful idea," Pru agrees, and Ruby nods.

"Yes, I think so too. Let's go then."

Tia starts to argue, but Tatiana and Ruby just grab her arm and drag her to the elevator, hushing her for the second time today. She starts to spark, and we all give her a wide berth in the small space. She crosses her arms and huffs but doesn't argue, and when we get to the lobby, everyone takes off. Taylor strips down again and changes. The girls are so distracted by everything they have learned that they don't make any dirty comments. Regan gathers his clothes, and the four witches teleport in a flash, leaving just me and the reluctant witch.

I smile at her. "Come on, my lady, your carriage awaits." I scoop her up in my arms, and she giggles as I walk toward the automatic doors, which open with a whoosh. "Hang on," I tell her, and her arms come up around my neck.

"Lucas." She looks into my eyes, and I see how serious she is. "Promise me you won't let me kill my grandfather."

I nod solemnly to her. "I promise I won't," I reply, but I also don't promise that I won't do it myself. I step off the entrance and start running, the wind rushing past our bodies as I speed us in the direction of her family home. Her body grows more and more tense the closer we get.

CHAPTER
Six

Tia

E verything just clicked into place after Tatiana
said and Ruby confirmed that I have a spell on
me. Memories that had been locked away of
my grandfather performing a yearly spell on my mother
and me instantly appeared in my mind. I remember
kicking and screaming and my mother pleading with
him to leave us be, the heavy feeling of despair
weighing me down, the pain every time I tried to use
my magic, and my mother's indifference to me. All of it
could have been avoided, and my life could have been
so much different if that man had died just before I was
born and not my grandmother. His bitterness over my
grandmother's death and the grudge that he seemed to
hold against me and my mother for whatever unknown
reason has been a plague on our lives.

I barely listen to the conversation as my mind runs
over everything I just learned. What little magic I have

sparks and fizzles across the top of my skin as outrage flows through my body—or maybe it's my locked away magic desperately trying to break free. Finally, I can get some answers, but first we need to wait while the guys investigate a missing human, something that could be detrimental to the coven and our continued manage-ment of the Earth portal. As much as I don't want to be on this island, my friends do, and I don't want anything to jeopardize that.

"Come on then, let's get to the bottom of this so we can help Tia with her problems." Lucas's smooth timbre saying my name jolts me out of my funk, and I watch as the three men use the elevator to get down to the portal room.

"What's going on?" I ask, slightly embarrassed that I have no clue. Ruby pulls out her phone and calls some-one, while Tati leads me over to the bar and helps me up onto a seat.

"The guys are going to check the security footage, and we are going to have a drink while we wait for them to return. Ruby is calling Pru."

"Mom, I need you to come to the manor right now," Ruby says as Tati goes around to the other side of the bar and pulls some premixed drinks out of the fridge. She pops the top and slides one over to me. "Here, you look like you could use this."

I blink at the pink bottled drink before waving my hand at the tequila bottle on the shelf. "That one please," I tell Tatiana.

She waves her hand, and the tequila bottle floats over, followed by a shot glass. I pour myself a shot of the yellow liquid before throwing it back.

"No, now. Damn it, Mom. This is serious. The tequila has come out." Ruby hangs up the phone and shakes her head. "Mom's on her way. I guess Tati and I should have one of those too," she says, sliding onto the seat next to me and slapping her hand on the bar. "A shot glass, good bar wench," she bellows, and Tatiana rolls her eyes before flipping her off, but she grabs two more glasses, and they both throw back a shot before Tatiana pours another round.

I don't even flinch as that one goes down, but I release the big breath I'd been holding.

"Okay, so yeah," Ruby begins awkwardly. "I guess this has to be a bit of a shock."

I shake my head and pick up the pink bottle, downing half in one go before wiping my mouth with the back of my hand.

"No, I think I knew all along, but there was something keeping me from saying anything, and I think it's the same for Mom," I tell them both quietly, and Ruby swears, but Tatiana just reaches out and grabs my hand.

"It's okay, Tia. We'll get to the bottom of this. Your grandfather will be punished, and hopefully we can free you both from whatever he's done to you."

"What if we can't?" I ask, my voice barely audible, but both Ruby and Tatiana hear it.

"No, no way," Ruby vehemently denies. "I'll call Nana and ask her if we have to."

"And I'll go back into the fae realm and ask Master Alsorin for his help. There is no way Mr. Lee is better than all of us. He's just been lucky because he did it in secret. I wouldn't want to be him now that Pru knows."

"Now that Pru knows what?" The head of our coven

steps out of the elevator, followed by Laura Woods. The Woods family owns both the Laughing Hamster and the Crafty Critters craft store. James has turned over the running of the Hamster to his son, Joshua, but Laura still runs the craft store.

"Holy shit, that was quick!" Ruby exclaims, looking down at her phone, which she tossed onto the bench countertop before taking her shot.

"Well, you said tequila was involved, so here we are. We dropped the invitations to Feasts and Fireworks and teleported right over." Pru purses her lips and looks between the three of us. "Right, better pour us a shot too," she tells Tatiana, coming over and wrapping her arms around me. Her familiar violet scent surrounds me, and I'm instantly transported back to a sad and depressed teen with no magic. Pru was often a comfort when I found none with my own mom.

"Hi, Pru," I mumble into her shoulder.

"Tia, darling, you are as beautiful as the day you left. We have missed you so," she says, pulling back and patting my cheek. She moves to the side, and Laura takes her place, hugging me tight.

"Hopefully now that you're back, we may see your mother more often. She attended the last coven meeting where we did the big spell, but that was because Pru wouldn't take no for an answer. It was the first time we'd seen her in a very long time," Laura tells me as she, too, takes a seat, and Tatiana passes them a shot. Both women throw them back. "And it makes me hopeful that my Estrella will be one of the next to return."

Estrella and Fiona had somewhat of a falling out

when Fiona declared tattooing unartistic. Much like me, Estrella left the island and made her own way in life. Laura has come to regret her harsh words, or that's what Ruby told me on the trip back to the island. I just hope she gets a chance to mend her relationship with her daughter like I now hope to mend mine with my mother.

"Okay, tell me everything," Pru demands, and so we spend the next half hour filling her in on everything we have found out and also why the guys are down in the portal room, checking the security footage. Pru grows steadily more irate the further along we get in the story, so when the guys finally return, she is sparking with fury as well.

After a small discussion, the decision is made to go out to my family farm and sort the immediate coven problem before Lucas heads to the vampire realm to hopefully take care of the greater coven issue.

"Right, shall we go? If we head down to the lobby, we can teleport to Blackwell farm," Pru suggests, and Taylor shudders and shakes his head.

"Nope, I'll run. Teleporting does bad things to my tiger."

"And I can't teleport," I remind them, but a small part of me hopes that's about to change. Everything will be different if I have powers. A small part of me is hopeful for the first time in so long, but not too hopeful. I'll be devastated if my lack of powers isn't caused by a spell.

"I'll carry you," Lucas offers, stepping forward suddenly, and my heart speeds up so fast, I worry it's going to beat out of my chest.

Ruby's and Pru's heads swivel almost identically as they turn to look at the poor mayor, their gazes narrowed. Lucas grimaces and looks like he's swallowed a lemon under their intense stares, but he stands his ground. Brave vampire.

"Yes, that is a wonderful idea," Pru agrees, and Ruby nods.

"Yes, I think so too. Let's go then."

"Hang on second, what's he going to do, haul me around like I'm a sack of wheat?" I argue, but my friends grab me firmly by the arms and drag me toward the elevator, hushing me once more. I grit my teeth and only just resist stomping my foot. Damn bossy bitches. I feel my power spark across my skin once more, and everyone steps back, giving me plenty of room in the small elevator.

When we get to the lobby, the others take off. Taylor strips down again and changes before bounding out of the hotel. Regan gathers his clothes, and the five witches teleport in a flash, leaving just me and the sexy vampire mayor.

I look at him, but before I can say anything, he smiles, flashing a hint of fang, and I lose my train of thought. "Come on, my lady, your carriage awaits." He scoops me up, and I can't stop a giggle from escaping. I'm equally terrified and excited about what's about to happen, both out at the farm and in this man's arms.

When we get outside, he looks down at me, his breath washing across my face. It's minty fresh and not at all what I was expecting from a blood drinker. I'm also not sure why I'm thinking like that.

"Hang on," he warns me, and I wrap my arms tightly around him.

"Lucas," I say quietly, and his gaze doesn't leave mine. "Promise me you won't let me kill my grandfather." I need to know that someone will temper my fury, because I don't trust any of the witches. They will be just as angry as me, and I have no doubt that they would also kill that man if anyone let us. There is nothing like a witch scorned or betrayed.

"I promise I won't," he assures me, and I believe him, except I can't help but notice the manic glint in his eyes. I don't think my grandfather is going to be safe from any of his visitors.

We arrive in a rush of wind, and I keep my eyes closed as I try to regain my equilibrium and not to vomit on the very sexy mayor. When he puts me down and holds me as I get my balance, I open my eyes and gasp at what I see.

From the looks of everyone else, they also appear to be completely stunned by the state of my family farm. What used to be a pretty white clapboard cottage is now a flaking, gray, broken shuttered dump. The gardens, which used to be immaculate, are filled with weeds and unkempt, and the grounds surrounding the cottage are now a barren wasteland. We always had a good buffer of forest between our cottage and grandfather's workspace just in case, but now all that remains are dead skeletons of the trees.

"What happened here?" Ruby whispers as Taylor's tiger runs down the driveway. Regan holds out his clothes, and he grabs them and runs behind a nearby garden shed, which is in the same condition as the rest of the place.

"My mother used to love gardening. It was the one time she almost seemed normal. My grandmother had an affinity with nature, and Mom seemed to follow her line of abilities and not Grandfather's."

"The magic is unhappy," Laura murmurs as she reaches out, and I feel her own magic spark before she pulls her hand back quickly. "Very unhappy." She and Pru exchange a loaded glance.

The front door to the house bangs open, and my grandfather steps out, brandishing a shotgun. I gasp at his appearance. The once strong and proud Chinese man is a withered husk. His clothes are hanging off him, so much so that he's swimming in them, and his hair has turned gray.

"Why is he pointing a gun at us?" Taylor asks conversationally as he steps out from behind the shed, wearing his clothes once again.

Grandfather steps out into the light, his gaze skimming the crowd. He sneers at the coven members before his eyes fall on Lucas and narrow. "What have I told you, you bloodsucking leech? You're not welcome here, and I said I would make your life unpleasant if you returned." He lowers the gun, sighting it up, but Lucas doesn't flinch. We just watch as Pru raises a hand and the barrel of Grandfather's gun melts, leaving it useless.

"It looks to me like Chen's magic is failing him. It doesn't like to be used maliciously. Is that what is happening, Chen? You no longer have magic so you have to rely on human weapons?"

My grandfather throws the gun on the ground in disgust. "I have enough magic to take care of that bloodsucker." His hands spark, but it's nothing like the well of power he used to have.

Pru chuckles, and Grandfather sneers at her. "I think that maybe you overestimate your power, Chen. It barely feels like a ripple of what it used to be. You are being punished, but why is that?"

Grandfather splutters out curses, and my eyes widen. That's not like him at all. He thinks swear words are for idiots. It's like the man is devolving. I take that moment to step forward, and when he sees me, his eyes bulge and he turns red.

"You."

"Hello, Grandfather," I say calmly despite my racing heart and shaking hands, which I hold behind me. "I wish I could say it was nice to see you, but I can't, and it never has been."

He raises his hand, and power streams out of it and directly toward me. It's a pure black bolt aiming straight for my heart. I'm so surprised at this ferocious, hostile attack that I freeze. It's like everything is in slow motion. Pru swears and utters a counterspell, her golden stream of magic racing to stop Grandfather's at the same time I feel arms wrap around me and move me out of the line of fire just in time. The two powers collide, and they explode. Lucas shields my body from the fallout, grunting in pain as his back gets peppered with the exploding power. Luckily Pru's power diffuses Grandfather's, making it benign, but it still isn't comfortable for the poor man who just saved my life.

Meanwhile, Ruby reacted and froze my grandfather. He is unable to move or cast, but he can still speak, unfortunately. He spews so much vitriol and hate that we are all momentarily stunned.

"Are you okay?" Lucas holds me at arm's length and runs his eyes over me. He has a cut on his cheek that is bleeding, and his arms are also sliced up from the exploding spell.

"I'm fine," I tell him before doing my own inspection, and just like I guessed, his back is sliced up too. I gasp and put my hand over my mouth at the sight of his torn shirt, blood seeping through all the cuts. "Oh my god. What did he do to you?" I run a finger over one of the cuts, strangely captivated by the color of his blood. He flinches, and I shake myself out of my weird trance.

"Crap, man, do you need blood?" Taylor asks him, and Lucas shrugs.

"Yeah, I've got some back in the fridge at home. It will be fine. I'll take care of it when we're done here."

"Absolutely not. I can have it here in seconds," Pru says, but I hold up my hand, stopping her.

"Wait, he can have my blood. It's the least I can do to repay him for protecting me." Lucas's pupils blow out as I offer him my wrist.

My grandfather starts to scream. "Of course you're a whore just like your mother, throwing yourself at bloodsucking trash."

"Right, how about we take Mr. Lee inside and let

them have some privacy?" Regan seems to be a little uncomfortable as he herds everyone inside. Pru waves a hand and moves my grandfather, who is still yelling obscenities at me.

Tatiana stops and places her hand on my wrist, looking at Lucas. "You make sure you tell her exactly what's going to happen when you take her blood." She sounds fierce, and I feel my eyebrows jump in surprise. What is she talking about?

Lucas nods, almost looking annoyed. "Of course I will. I'm not some teenager trying to score."

She stares him down before she decides he's telling her the truth then drops my hand. "We'll look for your mom. I don't like this at all," she tells me.

"We'll be in as soon as Lucas is better," I reply, torn between helping the man who saved my life and looking for my mother who may also need to be rescued, but I know my coven will look after her.

Tatiana hurries inside, leaving us alone.

CHAPTER
Seven

Tia

I turn to look at my savior, and he sees way more than I want him to.

"It's okay, Tia, I can wait. We can go find your mother," Lucas reassures me and goes to step away, but he staggers, and I leap for him, trying to steady him. He's too heavy, though, and I can't support him, so we slide to the ground. I break his fall with my body.

"Oomph." The air whooshes out of my lungs, and Lucas grunts. "Okay, my ass," I grumble as I get us sorted. I feel like an old-world damsel with a wounded soldier lying on my lap. "Here, drink." I hold out my wrist, and his eyes turn red and his fangs grow like they did earlier when Kadir asked to see them. He gently takes my wrist and turns it over so the inside is facing him. He leans in and runs it against his nose, inhaling deeply, and his eyes narrow slightly in thought before he looks at me.

"Do you know anything about how a vampire feeds?" he asks me, and I shake my head.

"No, just that you need blood to recover from an injury like that."

"Yes, blood helps us regenerate, and without it, we wither," he tells me, rubbing his thumb back and forth across the pulse in my wrist. The movement is soothing, and I feel my heart rate start to slow.

"You don't die?" I ask, distracted by his hypnotic movements.

He shakes his head. "No, we become a husk like a mummy, but we don't die. Only a stake through the heart with a specific type of wood will kill us. Not even beheading us will kill us. We just go into a sort of stasis until we can get blood and our body parts are put back together."

I shudder at what he describes. I could think of nothing worse than being alive forever in pieces.

"So blood is needed, and we mostly feed from bags if we are unattached. Those with partners can feed from one another. We have created a synthetic blood that will suffice, but it is no substitute for feeding from a partner, which is an intimate and erotic experience. My venom will make you orgasm, which is what Tatiana wanted me to tell you before I fed."

My eyes widen with surprise. "How does Tatiana know this?" I ask, and he chuckles.

"That's her story to tell, but she and Regan had a very interesting experience when they were in the vampire realm." His grin drops. "This is why I suggested that I can feed from my bags at home."

I consider everything he's told me, and I can hardly

deny him just because him feeding from me is going to give me an orgasm. God knows no other man has in a long time.

"It's fine, Lucas. Are there any other side effects? Am I going to force myself on you or anything."

"No. It will be a very pleasant experience for you. It's actually a survival mechanism. Not many people say no to being bitten when they get something out of it too."

A wry smile crosses my lips. "I can imagine."

"You honor me with your trust," he says as he leans in and licks a line across my veins. "My saliva has anesthetic and healing properties, so you shouldn't feel a thing." His eyes hold mine as he leans in and bites down. I watch his fangs pierce my body, but I feel nothing. He then removes them and presses his lips around the two holes in my skin and starts sucking.

Holy fuck, it's like he's sucking directly on my clit. My back bows, and I moan loudly, the sound obscene in the quiet front yard. His eyes widen, and he sucks harder, his grip on my wrist tightening as he, too, moans loudly. Like a rolling wave, the orgasm flows through my body, igniting every nerve ending, and I scream as I explode. I clench my thighs together and squeeze my eyes shut, wishing he was buried deep inside me instead of still reclining on my lap. I want to feel his thick cock pounding into me like he can't get enough. I want him buried so deep I don't know where I end and he starts. I hear his name cross my lips, which is enough to jolt him out of his own trance. He pulls away, swiping his tongue over the puncture wounds, and I watch in amazement as they close up in front of my very eyes. There's a drop of blood on the corner of his mouth, and he uses his tongue to catch it. He's frowning, and I worry that I've done something wrong.

Before I can ask what's wrong, Lucas speaks. "You're not just a witch, Tia. You're part vampire, I can taste it in your blood."

I am unable to even comprehend such a weird statement before the door to the house slams open and my mother comes running out, drawing our attention.

"No, don't let him drink from you," she screams, her hair in disarray and her too baggy shirt slipping off her shoulder. She looks unkempt, like she hasn't showered in weeks, but when she looks at my wrist, she knows she's too late. She sags against the side of the house and drops her head into her hands. "I'm so tired of all the secrets. Come inside, we have a lot to talk about," she says without looking at either of us, then she pushes off the house and walks back inside, leaving us alone once more.

Holy crap, that's the most animated my mother has ever been. What happened in there? I look from where she was to the gorgeous man in front of me who's still staring at me in both puzzlement and wonder.

"Ah, did you say I am part vampire?" I ask him, and he gets to his feet, all of his injuries healed. He holds out a hand and helps me up. I sway a little, and he wraps an arm around my waist.

"Steady, I took quite a bit. I was more damaged than I realized," he apologizes and helps me into the house.

We find everyone gathered in the living room. My grandfather is still bound, but there is now a gag across his mouth, and my mom is standing in front of him, brandishing her wand. It's sparking with black death magic, and Pru and Laura have hold of her arms.

"No, Fiona, not like this," Pru says in a commanding voice.

"What's going on?" I whisper to Ruby who is standing back, watching the action with a damn bag of popcorn in her hand.

"Shh," she hushes me again, and I want to throttle her, but Lucas's hand squeezes my waist, and I instantly feel calm again. "When we got in here, your mom was sitting on the couch, and she didn't even look up. It was like she was in a trance. My mom and Laura joined hands and chanted something, and all of a sudden, it was like a switch was flipped, and your mom was normal again. She asked where you were then went running outside. When she came back, she conjured that wand, and now she is threatening your grandfather with death. Dude, this is better than some telenovela." She crunches another mouthful of popcorn, and I turn my attention back to the scene before us.

"You racist, bigoted piece of shit. You couldn't just be happy that I found the love of my life. No, because he was someone you didn't approve of, you had to take matters into your own hand. Fuck! You even tried to kill your own grandbaby when she was still in my womb. Only Mother stepping between us stopped you, but you killed her instead," my mother sneers, the hatred in her voice making me shiver along with what she just announced.

The whole room gasps at this bit of information. We'd always been told that grandmother had had a sudden stroke and died before paramedics could get here.

"What did you do with Jarlen? I know he didn't just disappear. We were going to get married and move to the vampire realm and live there with his sons."

Lucas freezes next to me, and every single muscle in his body tightens like he's getting ready to pounce at my mother's words.

"Jarlen?" Pru tips her head to the side. "King Jarlen? Fiona, honey, put the wand down and please tell the rest of us what is going on."

Laura waves a hand and opens the coat closet, and then with her other hand, she magically pushes my grandfather into it before closing it again. She claps her hands together. "There, that will hold him while you tell us everything." She waves her fingers, and the bottle of tequila we'd been drinking at the manor appears on the coffee table. "I have a feeling we're going to need this."

My mother sags in defeat and lets her wand disappear before she turns to me, tears streaking down her face. "My baby, how I've missed you." She holds out her arms, and Lucas lets me go, giving me a little push in her direction. My steps start off slow, but within seconds, I'm rushing toward her. Her arms wrap around me, and we sob, words tumbling out of both our mouths, neither really hearing the other as we make up for so many years.

I can hear the others murmuring behind me, but I pay no attention to them, because my focus is on the woman in front of me. "Mama, I missed you," I mutter, and she pulls away and grasps my face with both hands.

"You've turned into such a beautiful woman. We have so much to talk about. I'm so sorry that I was not able to overcome that man. He's basically kept me captive from the day you were conceived."

"Come and sit. Tell us everything," Pru encourages, and when we turn, we find Pru and Laura on the sofa.

Laura pats the space between them. "Come and sit here, Fiona. Pru and I want to funnel some more magic into you to help with the magic waste. We'll have you back to normal in no time."

"You sit there, Tia." Pru points to the sofa opposite where Lucas happens to be sitting. Regan, Taylor, Ruby, and Tatiana have all retrieved seats from the dining table and brought them into the room.

I'm reluctant to let go of my mom, but I need to hear her story, our story, so we separate. I take the place next to Lucas, his body radiating warmth, and I feel comforted by it. He reaches for my hand and gives it a squeeze.

My mother doesn't take a seat. Instead, she grabs a shot of tequila and throws it back. She shudders at the taste, her nose wrinkling much like mine does before she starts pacing back and forth.

"Where do I start? I guess I can do this. There's no need for me to be spelled now that this is all going to come out." My mom lifts a hand and waves it across her face and down her body. She shimmers as a spell lifts itself, and when she is revealed, none of us can stop the gasps and exclamations of surprise.

"Holy fuck!" Pru swears, and she gapes at my mom who now looks like she's reverted to my age. Gone are the gray streaks and fine wrinkles, and in their place are luscious black locks and smooth golden skin. My mom and I could be twins. "What kind of spell was that and how can I do the same thing?" she demands, and my mother chuckles, but it's Lucas who answers.

"You're a vampire, or part vampire, aren't you? You stopped aging when you became someone's mate."

My mom smiles at him and nods. "Yes, I am and I did." She turns to Pru. "Sorry, it isn't a spell, it is the result of my mating with Jarlen."

Pru and Laura exchange a glance before they both grin. "You dirty bird. We never knew you had it in you," Laura teases, and Pru looks thoughtful.

"If I remember correctly, that was just before he disappeared. He had been here for a full moon celebration, and I remember the two of you immediately hit it off and were inseparable for weeks. We took bets on how long it would be before you moved to the vamp realm."

"Yes, Jarlen and I were mates. When we slept together that night of the full moon, the mating bond clicked into place. I was going to live in the vampire realm, but you know how my dad is, so we spent a few weeks here on Morbank, trying to get him used to the idea."

"That obviously didn't work out how you wanted," Taylor says. All four of them have popcorn now, and I have the urge to strangle Ruby, but Lucas still has hold of my hand.

"Well, at first he pretended that he was happy for me. I think it was for my mother's sake. She thought it was a blessing for me to find a mate. Most witches are very accepting of other supernaturals, and the Arbor

Vitae Coven has always preached acceptance and understanding, but the coven my grandfather came from wasn't as tolerant. They think that vampires and shifters are animals ruled by their baser needs, and that the fae are an oversexualized bunch of deviants."

"Yes, I remember some of his rants when he would come to coven meetings after your mother's death, Fiona. He certainly didn't hold his tongue. That is why I stopped insisting on his attendance." Pru shakes her head with sadness.

"Well, Jarlen and I discovered we were expecting, and we were overjoyed. I insisted that we should return home to the vampire realm so his child could be born there. They were going to be half vampire and would need to go through their vampire awakening." My hand tightens in Lucas's as I realize she's talking about me.

"We went home to tell Mom and Dad we were leaving, and he was waiting for us. He must have been planning it since he first found out, because he had procured a spell—a fae spell, not a witch one—to immobilize a vampire. When we announced we were pregnant and leaving, he used that spell and then staked Jarlen. He then turned on me and tried to kill the baby growing in my stomach. That's when my mother stepped between us, and he killed her instead. He was incensed, and then he used the forbidden puppet spell on me."

The Millers all gasp, and Regan looks fairly ill.

"What spell is that? I've never heard of it," Laura asks.

Ruby answers, "It's a forbidden spell. The only

reason we know of it is because Nana taught us to look for it. Shit, that's what was on Fiona? That's horrible."

"A puppet spell allows the wielder to control the person they cast it on, and when they are not being controlled, they are basically in stasis, which is how you were when we arrived," Pru explains, and my mother nods.

"Yes, the two of you combining power was enough to overpower my father. Thankfully his magic has been getting weaker and weaker each year."

"But what about the spell on Tia? What is that? And how come I was able to talk to you when I saw you? I asked you about Tia all the time." Ruby sounds confused, and Mom shrugs.

"That was all Chen. He said if I didn't pretend, he would track Tia down and force her to come back, so I told you things you wanted to hear, and it kept him happy. I'm sorry, but I was protecting my child. I believe the spell on Tia is a power dampening spell. I think my father believed that if she had no power, then her vampire traits would not appear either. He couldn't try to kill her again, because my mother's sacrifice gave her protection against that."

"Like Harry Potter?" Taylor points out, and my mother frowns.

"Who?"

"Hush, Taylor, Fiona probably doesn't know who that is," Tatiana hisses at him, and he blushes.

"It's a movie, Mom, one where the mother puts herself between her child and death magic, and because of her love, he gains protection," I explain, and my mother nods vigorously.

"Yes, that's actually right. My mother's sacrifice made it so my father could not kill you again, and he couldn't use the puppet spell on you. His only option was to contain your magic."

"I have magic?" My voice is small as it all sinks in. I have magic.

"And a vampire papa," Ruby says conversationally, her eyes sparkling with delight.

"No, she *had* a vampire papa. Chen killed him," my mother murmurs, the grief in her voice immense.

CHAPTER
Eight

Lucas

I hear the sadness in Fiona's voice. I was not surprised when she revealed her true form to everyone else, since I had already tasted the truth in Tia's blood, but to hear her name our missing king as Tia's father was a huge surprise.

We knew he had gone missing not long after attending the coven's full moon celebration. He'd been restless and searching for his true mate, and had been venturing to the other realms in the hope that she may appear. The coven was suspected of foul play at first, but they were quickly cleared when he was sighted in the fae realm, and then our search turned in that direction. The trail led us on a wild goose chase that eventually went cold, and I now no longer doubt that the warlock stuffed into the closet had something to do with that. I'm assuming he had help, though, and if he had a fae spell to immobilize him, I'm guessing someone in the fae realm assisted.

"How were you able to feed?" I ask her, and she shrugs.

"My father knew that I had to drink blood and provided one bag a month."

My mouth drops open in shock. "One bag a month? How did you not attack anyone?" I ask incredulously. "How are you not attacking anyone now?"

"I'm holding on by a thread. It's only the thought of hurting my friends and my daughter that keeps me from going feral," she admits, not meeting anyone's gaze.

"Pru. The fridge in my apartment is full of blood bags, can you bring them here?" I ask her, and with a wave of her hand, they appear on the coffee table in front of us. I stand and gather them into my arms. "Come on, we'll get this taken care of before we go any further."

"Is that not enough? You'll have to enlighten us non-blood drinkers," Tia calls out and follows us into the kitchen. I don't point out that once she has her vampire awakening, she will also be drinking blood. I think that would be beyond her limit of comprehension, however, and I don't want to scare her.

"No, I drink a bag a day," I tell her, and her eyes widen as she comprehends that her grandfather had basically been starving her mother.

"It's why I could never fight him or the puppet spell. Apart from his firework magic, he is a fairly weak warlock, but by starving me, he prevented me from fighting back. He kept me alive because he was too vindictive to kill me. He wanted to see me suffer and gloat about how he was able to defeat me and the almighty vampire king." Fiona sounds disgusted, and another tear trickles down her cheek.

I quickly pour one of the bags of blood into a mug and microwave it for her before passing her the cup. She all but snatches it out of my hand and drinks it so fast I don't have time to warm another before she's finished. She wipes the blood from her mouth with the back of her hand, looking a little sheepish.

"I haven't had warm blood since Jarlen and I mated. I'm sorry," she apologizes, looking ashamed, and I shake my head.

"Fiona, your self-control is astounding. Most of us would be ripping our family and friends apart if we'd been starved like you have. It's one rule that is pummeled into vampire children when we are young— do not allow yourself to get hungry." I pass her the next mug, and Tia takes the empty one from her. Fiona flinches slightly and shields her mouth, hiding her fangs, but her daughter just smiles and pulls her hand away.

"It's okay, Mom. This is what you are now. There's nothing wrong with it." A sense of relief washes over me. If Tia can handle watching her mother drink blood from the cup and me drinking it from her wrist, then maybe when she realizes she will be drinking blood as well, she won't freak out as much.

Fiona drinks five bags before she stops. She pats her stomach and groans. "Ugh, I don't think I've ever felt so full." She leans against the kitchen counter, and I clean up the mess, washing out the cups, disposing of the empty bags, and putting the other ones in the fridge for her.

"There are ten more. I have to travel back to the vampire realm in a couple of days, and I will arrange to double my order so that when mine gets delivered, some will be delivered for you too," I tell her as her eyes slide to the side, looking at her daughter who is drying the mugs we used.

I nod my head slightly at the unspoken words, and Fiona sighs with relief. She realizes what has to happen for Tia. If it doesn't, I'm not sure what will ensue. When the spell blocking her powers is lifted, her starved and dormant vampire side may just break through. I've never heard of a vampire who didn't go through their awakening, so this is a new thing we have to worry about. If only her father were here, because he would know what to do.

We move back out to the living area where we left the others. They are talking quietly, but all fall silent when we return.

"Feeling better?" Regan asks, and Fiona smiles at him.

"Yes, thank you, Regan. Thank you, all of you. Thank you for bringing my girl home, Ruby. Thank you for finally seeing my father for the horrid man he is," Fiona gushes, and there are so many emotions in her words.

Pru waves her hand. "Oh, we always knew he was horrid, we just had no idea he was pure evil." She stands up and walks over to her friend. "Can you ever forgive me?"

"Us," Laura chimes in.

"For not paying enough attention?" Pru finishes, and Fiona stops her.

"There is nothing to forgive. When I was out in public, I didn't dare defy him. He watched me everywhere. I wasn't going to risk Tia's life again." Fiona beams at her daughter. "I would have done anything to keep her safe, and there wasn't much I could do at home. Every time I tried to fight my way through the spell, he would recast it."

"The puppet spell needs to be tied to an object for it to work. Where did he get an object that would hold that kind of power? Certainly not from any of the witches from this coven," Pru asks.

"Yes, it's the charm that hangs around his neck. I'm not sure where he got it from. He used to ramble all the time. I think his mind is failing because the dark magic is eating away at it, but he mentioned a warlock friend with access to the realms and connections with some sketchy fae and vampires. Wouldn't that have to be someone in our coven? There's no way father would have dealt directly with *lesser beings*." Fiona sneers the last bit in a parody of her father.

Pru's eyes flash, and her hair lifts. "I wonder if that would be William. He certainly is on our shit list today. I think a visit to him won't wait. We'll go there next."

"As long as you take him into custody. I don't want him to get word to his contacts in the vamp realm. I need to tell the kings everything so we can squash the blood trafficking operation," I tell Pru, who assures me that William will be put into custody and his magic blocked.

Fiona gasps. "Kings?"

"Yes, Jarlen's sons have ruled in his stead since Jarlen has been gone. They are good and wise kings… mostly." I mutter that last word, still pissed off at them for my sister's treatment, but then I start to chuckle. "Oh no, this is too good. You're their sister." I point at Tia. "And a princess of the vampire realm. Oh, they are not going to know what's hit them."

I laugh a little more, and Tia frowns with confusion, but then something Fiona says fully registers.

"Hang on, you said your father staked King Jarlen, but did you see his body crumble? What wood did he use?" I ask, feeling more and more excited.

Fiona frowns and shakes her head. "No, I didn't see it, but between my mother's death, the spell, and trying to protect my baby, I was distracted. Now that you mention it, he did not turn to ash. The last time I saw him, he was still immobilized by the spell with the wooden stake through his heart, but he was in one piece." Her eyes widen, and she looks at me with hopeful tears in her eyes. "Could he still be alive?"

I stand up. "There is only one wood that can kill a vampire, and it is a closely guarded secret. Unless Mr. Lee has access to that, and I doubt he did since those trees were eradicated years ago, then there is only a stockpile inside the royal vault for criminals and emergencies. He may still be alive, but where would he have stashed him?"

Fiona jumps to her feet as the others all burst into chatter.

"Yes, you're right. I'd forgotten all about that!" Pru exclaims, sounding excited.

"If we had something of his, we could do a locator

spell. Do you have anything, Fiona?" Laura asks, looking at Fiona.

"No, my father threw out anything that was remotely related to Jarlen years ago," she says sadly.

"I could shift and sniff him out," Taylor offers, but I shake my head.

"No, I doubt there would be any smell. Mr. Lee is smart enough to cover something like that despite his lack of visitors, and desiccating vampires don't really smell. They are dry husks."

"Desiccated?" Tatiana sounds shocked.

"Yes. When a vampire doesn't have access to blood, or they are staked through the heart by a wood other than the one that is lethal to us, we shrivel up and go into stasis. It's a defense mechanism. Sometimes vampires become bored with life and don't want to choose the final death, so instead they choose to sleep for periods of time."

Tatiana wrinkles her nose. "So he's alive but in stasis?"

"Yes," I confirm, and she heaves a sigh of relief.

"It would have been horrible for him to be awake all this time."

"The work shed," Tia says suddenly. "If he's anywhere, it will be there. Grandfather doesn't let anyone else into that space. When I was a child, if I even got too close, I would be punished. He claimed it was for my safety, but now that I know he tried to kill me, it must be for another reason. Come on, I'll show you."

She grabs my hand, and we exit the run-down cottage. I can hear voices following us, but I am on a single-minded mission to find my king at the moment.

I'm tempted to pick her up and carry her, but I don't know where we're going, so I let her lead. Plus, her hand feels nice in mine—so nice that I haven't wanted to release it since I fed from her. Tia Blackwell is even more intriguing to me now. Part witch, part vampire. She will need to go through her vampire awakening, but I'll let her father talk to her about that... if it turns out he is alive.

Tia leads me down a garden path that winds around the back of the house and farther into the dead forest. The barren forest stretches for miles. I sense more than see Fiona catch up to us. She has the grace and speed of a vampire, and Tia startles slightly.

"Slowly," she cautions us, holding up a hand. "My father is incredibly fond of booby traps."

Tia freezes on the spot. "That's new," she says, carefully looking around, and Fiona shakes her head.

"Actually, it's not. Somehow you always knew how to avoid them. It used to infuriate him," Fiona replies before telling me, "Let Tia lead." She pushes her daughter in front of us. "Use your instincts, they are never wrong. Your magic might be smothered, but it's still there. He has never been able to stamp it out completely, and the fact that it manifests in magical fireworks used to drives him wild. It would make my day when you would spark and fizzle in defiance."

We watch as Tia looks around, her magic sparking across her skin as she tries to feel out the magical traps.

"Pretty, isn't it, Mayor Sharpe?" Fiona says quietly.

"Very, and please call me Lucas."

"I know of you, of course," she says. "Jarlen told me all about his sons, nephew, and their best friend, and all the trouble you would get up to. You be very careful with my daughter's heart. She has been through too much, and I just want everything to be perfect from here on out."

I look down at Fiona who is a good head below me and put my hand over my heart. "I swear on my life that I will give her everything she deserves," I promise the woman who I have a feeling will be our next queen. She looks at me carefully, and I feel like those dark eyes can see directly into my soul, before she smiles gently.

"I believe you, but I will hurt you if you even so much as make her cry. I have had many years of plotting my father's demise, so I have gotten very creative," she promises, and I don't doubt her one bit.

Before she turns away, I can see her mulling something over in her head. I guess she decides she's brave enough to ask. "Lucas, the triplets' mother, is she still around?" I reach my hands out for hers, and I take them, giving them a squeeze.

"Lady Lyndsay remarried a few years ago. She found her own mate, and they have recently had triplet baby girls. She was never Jarlen's true love, just someone who he was comfortable enough to have an heir with. She just happened to give him three. She still visits with her sons and brings her daughters with her as far as I know, but she no longer lives at the palace, and she will be overjoyed that Jarlen is alive and has found his true love." My words obviously help, because some of the tension she'd been holding slides away.

"Okay, let's do this." She turns and begins to march forward, catching up with Tia who has started making a path through the remainder of the forest. Ruby is following behind, leaving a trail of magic for the others to follow safely.

We walk for a good ten minutes, the forest getting stragglier and more run-down the farther we go. The trees are covered with a disease that is green and oozing.

"What is this?" Taylor asks, picking up a branch and dragging it through the ooze.

"I have no idea," Laura answers.

Pru shrugs. "We should probably get Minerva and Meadow out here to have a look. They are the plant experts."

"And if they can't help, I know someone in the fae realm who might be able to," Tatiana says, and Pru grins.

"Would that be Master Alsorin? I heard Regan telling his dad that you met him when you were there."

"Yes, he was the one who gave me the potions for us girls."

"Now that is one good-looking powerful man who is very good with his hands." Pru fans herself, and Laura and Fiona giggle like school children.

"Eww, Mom, no," Ruby says, plugging her ears with her fingers, and the other coven children look a little grossed out, but Taylor can't help stirring the pot.

"Oh, you've met him? Do tell," he prompts, and Pru opens her mouth to launch into what I'm sure is a sordid tale that I'm guessing happened before her marriage and children, but I don't want them to get sidetracked.

"Let's save the tale for later and find my king," I suggest.

"Of course. I'll tell you later, Taylor," she promises, and he looks a little ill that his shit stirring is backfiring.

"There." Tia points to an open space that is barren and dry without even a tuft of shriveled up grass on it.

Fiona pushes forward, flanked by Laura and Pru, and all three witches pull wands out of the air.

"On three," Pru commands. Their wands spark with magic, and I step back. Only really big spells require the use of wands to channel magic. They chant something that I don't recognize, and in unison, they flick their wands. Magic flies through the air, hitting something solid about five yards in front of us before dispersing. Slowly, a building comes into sight as their magic eats through the cloaking spell.

"Grandfather's workspace," Tia announces with awe in her voice. I can't forget that this must be like her holy grail—the one place she dreamed of being and was never allowed.

"Well, come on then. Why are we waiting? Let's bust out a vamp." Ruby marches for the small door on the right of the warehouse that must be the length of a football field. "And Mom, maybe you should grab the rest of those blood bags. If he's in here, then he's going to be a little hungry."

CHAPTER
Nine

Tia

R uby kicks the door open with her foot and turns around and grins at us. "I always wanted to do that."

She goes to step inside, and I jump forward, stopping her. "No!"

She startles and blinks owlishly at me.

"Grandfather may have booby trapped the warehouse too. In fact, I can almost guarantee it. Send out some searching magic," I instruct her, and her eyes widen, and she swallows heavily before quickly following my instructions. We watch as a candy pink trickle of magic streams through the door. It doesn't get far before there's a flash and something explodes inside, causing Ruby to yelp and jump back.

She rubs at her hand and scowls. "Your grandfather is an asshole," she mutters, and Tatiana steps up to take over as Laura grabs Ruby's hand and chants a healing spell over it. My mother puts out her hand to stop Tatiana.

"Here, let me. I heal quickly, and it's my father, so I should be able to feel for them better." Mom steps into the warehouse, and I follow closely behind her. I feel Lucas at my back and hear the others shuffle in behind him.

I gasp as I look around the large, cavernous space. There are all kinds of supplies in here. It's a pyrotechnician's dream, to be honest, but it's unusual that he keeps everything together. Human pyrotechnic makers are always careful to keep the dangerous stuff separate. He must have spells keeping everything safe.

I watch as my mom's magic, which is light red in color, sweeps the room. It lights up many spells, but like I assumed, these are all protective ones designed to keep the people inside the room safe. No more booby traps are triggered, so it must have just been the one by the door, which makes sense.

"Okay, it's clear," she announces, and we all move farther in.

"Holy shit!" Taylor looks around, his nose twitching, and he sneezes. "That's a lot of gunpowder and chemicals."

He's not wrong. My grandfather has barrels and barrels of different components all lined up and spaced out around the cavernous warehouse.

"Does this space look bigger on the inside than on the outside?" Regan has put his hand up to shade his face so he can see farther into the structure. The bright sunlight streams in through the skylights directly above us, but they stop farther down the building, and the structure plunges into darkness.

"Yes, there is obviously some kind of spatial distortion spell on the building." Lucas hasn't moved from my side, but I can practically feel him vibrating with tension. I know he's desperate to look for his king, but he's trying to be respectful.

"My father used to test his products in here, so there is definitely a spell allowing him height as well. I think that's in the darkened portion." Mom points farther down where Regan was trying to see.

"Come on, I think we should spread out and look. There is a cellar where he would store all his finished pieces, so we should check that out. Just be careful if you use magic in here. A magical spark could set off a chain reaction," I warn, and everyone's eyes bulge. I guess none of them had considered that. "Grandfather used to work by witch light. There must be some around here somewhere," I say, noticing a small work desk off to the side. I hurry over to it and pull open the top drawer. Sure enough, some of the spelled stones are inside. I pick them up and pass them out. Ruby activates them before passing them on. Soon, they each have a glowing stone that emits no static electricity, so there's no risk of setting off any of the chemicals.

"Alright, let's split up," Pru commands. "If we find him, I can bring the blood here."

"If we find him, we're going to need a lot more blood than I have on hand," Lucas says dryly, but my mom shakes her head.

"No, what we have is fine, and then he can drink from me."

"Ah, of course. If you are mated, you should be able to revive him quicker than any bagged blood could. Even though bagged blood won't be palatable for him because you are mated, it will stop him from sucking you dry, especially since I don't have any enarac fruit here," Lucas explains, and I feel a momentary pang of panic.

"Oh, but I do," Tatiana pipes up. "I was going to see if she could make it more palatable."

My mother shudders. "If you can do that, then every half vampire mate will worship her. It is foul."

"We can bring it here then, it's no problem," Pru assures us.

Shit, if he's here, then I'm about to meet my father for the first time. Also, holy fuck, I'm part vampire. What does that mean for me? Am I going to have to drink blood? I've never had to before, though there was that strange moment when I was inspecting Lucas for injuries when I felt a strange craving for his.

My stomach rolls. I don't know if it's from nerves, excitement, or the possibility of drinking blood. It's all tangled up together.

Everyone spreads out.

"Come on. Grandfather's main workspace is farther down the warehouse. He has some storage space there too," I tell Lucas, and he walks beside me. I hear the others talking, their voices echoing through the cavernous room.

"How do you know all this? I thought you weren't allowed in here," Lucas asks, his heat at my back telling me how close he is to me. It's nice, because the skylights stop, plunging us into darkness, and it becomes chilly. I hold up the witch light, and it illuminates the path in front of us.

"I've only been in here once before. I think Grandfather wanted to show me everything I couldn't have just to spite me. He seemed to take joy from it now that I think about it." I come to a stop at his work bench. As usual, it's spotless. My grandfather abhorred messes.

I turn in a circle, a faint memory rubbing somewhere in my mind, urging me to keep looking. To the side of the work bench is a large cupboard, so large it's almost out of place. I pass the witch stone to Lucas and grab both door handles, yanking them open.

Lucas holds up the stone, illuminating the deep recesses of the cupboard, and a scream leaves my mouth before I can stop it. It's long and loud, and I have no doubt everyone else heard it. Lucas swears a blue streak beside me as we take in the shriveled, desiccated husk of a man, whose eyes are wide open and staring at us.

"Fuck! Hang on, Your Highness. We'll get you out of there." Lucas shoves the witch light back into my hand and steps into the cupboard, carefully lifting the man into his arms. I clap a hand over my mouth so another scream doesn't leave it and step away as Lucas helps him out of his prison. He looks so much like a mummy, I expect bits to start flaking off of him, but they don't. His eyes move so they don't leave my face, and he blinks a couple of times, but apart from that, he can't do anything.

"Oh my god, Jarlen." My mother arrives in a flash

and drops to her knees where Lucas laid his king on the ground. Without waiting, she brings her wrist up to her mouth and bites down on it. When she pulls it away, blood wells on her skin, and she dribbles it into the king's mouth.

She keeps having to bite into her wrist because it keeps healing over. The others arrive as she's doing this, and none of them are able to hide their disgust at what we found.

"Holy fuck, is he awake? I thought you said they went into stasis when they were staked," Regan says, and Lucas shrugs, looking furious. His fangs are flashing, and his eyes have turned red.

"I have no idea. There's no stake in his heart, so I'm guessing Mr. Lee removed it once he thought the king had wasted away enough that he wouldn't be a problem anymore. I think King Jarlen has been awake all this time."

"That sick fuck," Ruby spits out. "That would be torture."

"Pru, those bags would be a good idea now," Lucas grinds out from between clenched teeth as he watches Mom try to get the king to swallow. "If we can get one into him, Ms. Blackwell, then it might be enough to get him to latch on."

"Call me Fiona, and yes, okay, this is not working." Mom sounds despondent, and I get down on my knees and wrap an arm around her shoulders.

"It's okay, Mom, we'll save him."

"Oh, honey. Your father was so excited when we found out we were pregnant with you. It was one thing to think he was dead and you were growing up without him, but to know he was here all along... I feel wretched. How did I not know my mate was here? Shouldn't I have felt that he was still alive?" She looks to Lucas for answers, but he just shrugs helplessly.

"I'm guessing whatever your father did to you dulled that as well. You weren't mated all that long before it happened."

"Here." Pru holds out a blood bag.

Lucas takes it, and his eyebrows rise. "It's warm," he observes as he tears a hole in the top of it.

"I can't imagine there is anything worse than cold blood." Pru shudders. "It was easy enough to warm them in my hands with a little spell."

We watch as he dribbles a small, continuous stream into my father's mouth. Nothing happens to start with, and some of it just runs back out, but before too long, we can see the muscles in his neck start to work as his swallowing reflex comes back to life. My mother heaves a sigh of relief, and we watch as his face starts to plump ever so slightly.

"Let's get a couple more into him before you finish him off." Lucas holds his hand out for another bag, and Pru passes it to him, already having anticipated it. One by one, my father drinks the remaining ten bags of blood. His skin starts to plump up almost like we are watching a reverse time lapse video. It's strangely fascinating and disgusting at the same time. Finally, my mother gently pushes me out of the way.

"Would you all give us a moment?" she asks, not looking away from her mate.

"Ah, yup, sure, no problem." Regan awkwardly hustles everyone away.

I hear Pru asking why and Ruby hushing her.

"I'll explain it when we get outside, Mom."

Lucas gets to his feet and holds out a hand to help me up. I quickly accept it. There is no way I want to be around to see my mother orgasm. "Take your time, we'll wait back at the house."

Lucas hurries me out of the warehouse, and thankfully I don't hear anything that will scar me for life. We're quiet on the walk back to the cottage. I guess both of us are lost in our thoughts, but his hand doesn't leave mine, and I don't want it to. There's something about this man that calls to me, something that I should be questioning, but I've decided life is too short to worry about that sort of thing. Look at my mom and dad. They spent twenty-six years apart because of a crappy situation—all that time wasted.

"So, um, I guess I'm part vampire." I finally break the silence as we near the cottage, no longer able to hold back my thoughts.

Lucas nods. "Yes, probably more vampire than witch, if we really think about it. Your dad's full vampire, and your mom was changed when she became pregnant with you, so you're probably only a quarter witch."

"Why haven't I needed or craved blood?" I ask quietly, feeling a little embarrassed and unsure, and he stops walking.

"Vampires go through an awakening, a special ritual that triggers their bloodlust. This doesn't happen until they are in their mid-twenties, so you wouldn't have needed it until you turned twenty-five. Have you turned twenty-five or is it soon? You are probably lethargic and anemic, right?"

I nod, and the recent diagnosis instantly makes sense. "I turned twenty-five a few months ago."

"So that would be your vampire side making itself known. Have you been craving red meat, the bloodier the better?"

My mouth rounds into an O as all of my recent and quite disturbing behavior finally makes sense. My friends were disgusted last time we went out for dinner, and I ordered my steak as rare and bloody as it could possibly be.

"So without the ritual, that's all it will do. It's a safety measure, and I'm almost certain that the dampening spell you have on you is probably targeting your vampire side as much as it is your witch traits. Your grandfather seems to be the type of man who would want to stamp out any possible hint of another species."

"You're not wrong. So what happens during a vampire awakening?" My curiosity is totally getting the better of me, and now I need to know everything. "And do you think I'll still have weak magic seeing that I'm more vampire than witch? Do you think I'll have any magic?" The questions tumble out of my mouth, and Lucas chuckles, running a hand through his hair. The worry in his eyes melts away at all my questions, which makes me happy. Seeing him upset made me upset. Shit, how did this happen so quickly? How can I care so much about a person I literally just met?

"A vampire awakening is a very sensual experience. You never forget the person you took your first blood from. It's almost like losing your virginity." His voice drops, and the amusement in his eyes changes to heat.

"Except, unlike that, you are guaranteed an orgasm," I joke, and he smiles.

"Yes, you most definitely are. There are experienced vampires available specifically for vampire awakenings to help the new vampire through it."

"That's their job?" I ask, unable to hide the surprise in my voice.

"Yes, and they are revered amongst my kind. It's an honor to help our young through their transition, but you don't have to use one of them, and some don't. Some have partners already picked out, and some fumble their way through it together. It's completely up to each individual vampire."

"And I would have to choose one of these vampires to help me?"

His eyes narrow, and he steps closer to me, picking up my wrist and running his nose across my pulse as he breathes me in once more. "You could, or I could help you through it. I promise that I can make it very good for you."

I feel my heart rate pick up at the thought of this incredibly sexy vampire being my first, and I can't say I hate the idea. Before I can respond, however, shouting inside the cottage breaks through our private little bubble, and we both stiffen before hurrying up the steps and into the house.

Pru has dragged my grandfather back out of the closet and removed his gag, and he's the one who is spewing profanities.

"You will all pay for this. How dare you restrain me!

I have done nothing wrong. I have friends in high places."

"Mr. Lee, we found King Jarlen. It's all over. The vampires will require your death for what you did to their king," Taylor tells him, and Grandfather's eyes widen as he starts to struggle.

"And it will be painful and long. They might even change him into a vampire so they can kill him over and over again, or stake him like he did with the king and leave him to rot for eternity. I can't tell you how creative we can be when we've been wronged," Lucas says, his eyes flashing red in anger. I feel the urge to reach out and soothe him, but I think that will only incense Grandfather more, and he is already an alarming shade of purple.

"I'd rather die than be a vamp," Grandfather spits out, but he turned pale at the thought of being changed, and he's stopped struggling.

"Well, maybe if you cooperate, we can make sure that punishment is off the table," Lucas says carefully, and I can tell I'm not the only one who is surprised.

"What?" Ruby asks. "You're going to let him get away with all that he's done?"

"I'm sure if he lifted the spell off the vampire king's daughter, it would go a long way in assuring his leniency," he replies, and we finally realize what he's trying to do.

My grandfather's smirk is smug. "None of you could lift that spell, could you? That's because it's not a witch spell like the one on Fiona. My fae contact told me to tie that one to an object too."

"Speaking of which..." Pru darts in, rips the cord off

his neck, and passes it to Taylor who crushes the pendant in his fist with his shifter strength. It sparks and flashes, and a cloud of black magic disperses into the air. "That's one. What did you anchor Tia's spell to?"

CHAPTER
Ten

Tia

He starts to laugh, and he sounds completely unhinged. He throws his head back, and when he drops his chin again, his eyes are black. I flinch as he locks his gaze on me, but Lucas steps between us, blocking his view.

"Whoa!" Tatiana steps back, and Regan wraps his arms around her. Ruby and Taylor also shuffle out of the way.

"A dark entity." Laura steps closer to my grandfather, sounding completely fascinated. "Do you think he invited it in, or it took over because of his evil ways?" Laura asks Pru, who shrugs.

"Chen was never powerful enough for any of this. I say he invited him in, but where on earth did he learn that spell?"

"Probably the same place he learned the puppet

one," Ruby muses. "But all of those books were destroyed by a spell except for the one Nana has as an archivist for all the covens."

"You witches are so narrow-minded." Grandfather's voice has taken on a sibilant tone. "You are so arrogant that you forget you are not the only magic wielders in the realms." He looks down at his frozen, trapped body and frowns. "Now release me, and no harm will come to you."

Pru and Laura laugh. "Yeah, that's not how this is going to work." Laura shakes her head.

"No, you can't go anywhere because of our spell. You are trapped in Chen's body until we decide to release him, but if you cooperate, we will consider letting you go," Pru offers, and the dark entity's gaze comes back to me.

I push Lucas out of the way. I appreciate him wanting to protect me, and God knows I need it without a spark of my own power, but I'm sick of being scared and weak all because of this man.

"Fae would be the other magic wielders you're referring to. I took a fae counterspell, and it didn't help."

"That's because it's tied to an object. You break that object, and all of your power will come rushing back to you." He must have decided to cooperate.

"What is the object, and where is it?" I demand, stepping forward, and the being starts to chuckle.

"Ah, Chen's mind is so warped. Even though he hates vampires, he gave it to the one who helped him so there was never a chance it would be found, and your magic couldn't be released. He couldn't let your mother's talisman go, though, because he got a sick sense of satisfaction out of controlling her, but yours was just a power dampener. He couldn't do the puppet spell on you because of your grandmother's sacrifice."

"Which vampire has it? Who is the traitor to my people?" Lucas demands, his hands clenched tight like he's trying not to shake it out of the creature.

"The vampire was no one special, just someone with a grudge against the king for always shutting down his blood farms. It's the object that is ironic."

"I think I will be the judge of whether the vampire was someone special or not." The deep voice comes from the doorway. We all turn to look, and standing next to my mother is my father. He's all plumped up and looking like he could take on an army with how bright his virility is.

"My liege, I'm sorry we failed you. We looked for you, but your trail led to the fae realm. We found your amulet there, and we concluded it was fae trickery." Lucas falls to his knees and bows his head, and my father shakes his head, hurrying forward.

"No, my friend, do not bow to me. It is good to see you." My father hugs Lucas like a long-lost son. "No one is to blame other than the people involved, starting with him." My father glares at my grandfather, but the dark being inhabiting him doesn't seem concerned whatsoever, and he just smirks.

My father releases Lucas and turns to me. His eyes are the same shade as mine, and I feel like he is looking deep into my soul, but I stand my ground, refusing to back down from this man who practically oozes power and strength. A small smile spreads across his lips, but tears glisten in his eyes.

"My princess! You have grown into a beautiful woman. I'm just sorry I could not be here to see it." He takes my hands. "Hopefully we can make up for lost time and get to know one another." He doesn't push to hug me, just gives my hands a squeeze, and a lump develops in my throat.

"I'd like that," I tell him, grateful that he isn't making some big, dramatic deal out of this. I don't like public displays of emotion, it tends to freak me out, though I have become slightly used to it because of the rest of the witches, but in my family, it was not a thing.

"Good, but first, let's deal with this." He turns back to face the being inside my grandfather's body. "Now give me the name of the vampire who so grievously betrayed me and my family."

"His name was Silvan Salvator, and he has an almighty grudge against your family, not the least because you keep shutting down his blood farms," the being offers helpfully. "And he is the one who holds the object that will unbind your daughter's powers."

Lucas gasps when he hears the name of the one responsible. I look to him for an explanation. "Not only is he Cole's older brother, but he's also the king's nephew. He hasn't been seen in years. Cole's father was Jarlen's younger brother, and he was a nasty waste of a man who was bitter that he was the younger son. He tried to kill Jarlen and was executed for his crimes. Silvan disappeared and has been missing ever since. We thought he slunk off in shame, but what if he is just following in his father's footsteps?

"Silvan!" King Jarlen spits out. "He's as slippery as an eel. We have never been able to catch him."

"That's because he has fae help." The being chortles, enjoying all the chaos.

"What is the object?" I demand, stepping up next to my father.

The being smirks. "His ruling pendant." The being nods in my father's direction. "And it must be destroyed to release your power."

Lucas gasps. "No."

My father hangs his head. "So be it."

"What's so bad about that?" The rest of the witches have been happy to stay quiet now that my father has arrived, but Ruby is so freaking nosy. Thankfully, she asks the question we all want to know the answer to.

"A ruling pendant is made for a king's family at the start of his rule by our goddess and is passed down to each succeeding king. If it is ever broken, then that signals it is time for a new ruling family, and that the goddess isn't happy with the current reigning family." Lucas's eyes are full of sympathy as my mom wraps her arms around my father, giving him support.

"So because we need to break it so Tia can have her power back, that means your family loses its right to rule the vampires? That's stupid. It's not like it broke on its own. I'm sure your goddess will see what is directly in front of her and make things right. Things have a strange way of working themselves out. Look at this, it's the perfect example. " Pru doesn't hold back, and I can't control the snort that escapes at her overwhelming optimism, but my father shakes his head.

"Whatever happens, I am happy to give up my rule so that my daughter can have access to her power. We'll need to organize your vampire awakening too. Once we return to the vampire realm, you can meet the vampires who can help you through it and see if any of them appeal to you," he says gently.

I feel my cheeks heat with a blush, and I shuffle awkwardly on the spot. My mother leaves my father's side and hurries over to me.

"Baby, this has to happen. It's already late for you, so we don't know what will happen once we lift the dampener spell."

"Ah, yup. I know, it's just a lot to take in," I hedge, not wanting to explain the real reason I'm flushing. Thankfully Lucas stays quiet about his offer to help me through my awakening, because I'm not ready to talk about that with anyone at the moment.

"While this is all sickeningly fascinating, could you please release me now, as promised?" the dark being says, cocking my grandfather's head slightly to the side. "My fun here is obviously at an end, and I have better things to do than be stuck inside this dying old man."

"Hang on, what about the fae who was working with them as well? We need a name. Your pendant was found in their realm, deep in the Forest of Woe. It must have been a fae who took it there," Lucas demands, and the being purses my grandfather's lips.

"What's in it for me?"

"Your ability to breathe," Regan growls, and Tatiana puts a hand on his back to soothe him.

"Fine, no need to be aggressive." The being rolls my grandfather's eyes. "Now this is juicy. I can't wait to see what you do with this information."

"Get on with it," my mother snaps, having reached her limit on seeing her father acting as a puppet, even though that's what he did to her for so long. I see it as karma, and it's kind of poetic.

He sighs dramatically. "You are no fun. Prince Aven is the fae who helped Silvan and Chen with their nefarious plans, and he is also the one with the forbidden book of spells. Actually, he has a whole heap of spell books that are forbidden—fae, witch, angel, and demon."

"Shit." Tatiana and Regan exchange a loaded glance, and Pru sighs heavily.

"This does not bode well for our coven."

"No, it really doesn't. There was another witch at the meeting they had when they planned this out. They facilitated everything, but they were wearing a concealment spell, one that I could not see through. It could have been a male or female witch for all I know, but they want Morbank Island for themselves. They want to control the portal. They have big plans for it, and blood farming is just the beginning."

"Why are you telling us this?" Laura asks, and the being shrugs.

"I can no longer see this play out, so I would like to cause as much chaos as I can before I am kicked out of this body. Your awareness of the plan upsets everything," he admits gleefully.

"King Jarlen, if I may?" Pru inclines her head toward the king, who gestures regally.

"Go ahead, Pru. I'd like to have a little chat with Mr. Lee without his friend using him as a meat suit."

I wrinkle up my nose at my dad's phrasing. Gross.

"Fiona, if you wouldn't mind contributing your power for this spell, I'd appreciate it." My mom beams at Pru and practically skips over to join the rest of the witches.

"It will be my pleasure. You have no idea how much my power is itching to get even."

That catches the being's attention. "Wait, what? You said you would free me."

"And we will, we just didn't promise that you would still be in the human realm when it happened." Laura scowls at the being. "I'm sure Chen was rotten when he let you in, but we can't let you wreak havoc somewhere else."

Taylor steps back toward Lucas and me, giving the witches plenty of room. Pru conjures up a bundle of herbs, and I recognize sage, chamomile, and rue as she lights them and gestures for me to come over.

"Although your powers are still bound, you can help with this. Can you smudge your grandfather while we chant the spell?"

"Of course." I'm pleased to be able to help, and I take the herbs and start to wave them around my grandfather's body. The being begins to cough and fight his bonds, but it's no use, he's well and truly trapped. The smoke settles over him in a fine layer, and I toss the rest of the bundle into the empty fireplace for it to smolder out before stepping back.

The six of them join hands, and a dome of white light surrounds them—a protection barrier against negative energy. Pru starts chanting, and the being struggles harder.

"What are they doing?" Taylor asks, and I shrug.

"I'm not the witch to ask, I have no idea."

"It's a banishment spell. It should send the entity

back to wherever he came from, which is hopefully a realm far away," Jarlen explains.

"But how did it get here?" I ask. "I thought the portal was the only way to travel around the realms." The chanting gets louder, and the being starts to scream as my grandfather's eyes flicker back and forth between his normal color and pure black.

"Their realm is not connected to the portal, and they have no corporeal form unless they are invited into one. They have the ability to squeeze through occasional rifts in the fabric when there are big shifts in time and space, and then they float around until they can find someone to latch onto. They are attracted to negative energy, so Chen was basically a beacon for it. We have had them in the vampire realm on a couple of occasions as well. The coven has always assisted us in ridding ourselves of them in the past. Ruby's nana is an especially powerful witch and quite adept at doing it on her own."

The chanting reaches a crescendo, and with one last ear-splitting screech that sends Taylor, Lucas, and Jarlen to their knees with their enhanced hearing, a black cloud dissolves out of my grandpa and dissipates. Grandfather's head falls to his chest, and he groans.

"Is it gone?" I ask as I hurry to help Lucas back to his feet. Mom helps Jarlen, and Regan reaches out a hand for Taylor now that their protection barrier is down.

"Yes it is. Back to whatever primordial sludge it crawled out of," Pru announces.

"Is there a way to tell if someone is infected by a dark entity?" Tatiana asks, wrapping her arms around herself, looking shaken with everything that just transpired.

"Yes. If Chen touched selenite when he had been carrying the entity, it would have turned black. Its energy is too pure to be handled by someone with darkness in their spirit," Laura replies.

"Right, good to know. Maybe we should all start carrying it with us." Taylor brushes his hands off on his pants.

"It's not a bad idea. I will talk to Minerva. She will come up with a way for us to carry some with us," Laura says but nods at my loudly groaning grandfather who seems to be regaining his faculties. "What are we going to do with him?"

"He is all yours, King Jarlen, as an apology from our coven to you. Not that it makes up for what you suffered the last twenty-six years, but I hope it's a start. Do with him what you see fit. Now we will leave you be, we have another problem to take care of. Lucas, we will let you know what we find out from William if you wish to remain here."

"Thank you, Pru, I would. The dark entity shed a lot of light on the blood farming, which gives us a direction to follow, but we need to get the king back to the vampire realm as soon as possible. Could you authorize a trip for us, Regan?"

"Of course. I'll let Mac know. Goddess be with you all. I'm sure your sons will be happy to see you, King Jarlen. Good luck to you all."

"Here, do you want this?" Taylor offers the missing human's shirt to Lucas. It was tucked into his pocket the whole time. "You may be able to get a scent off it in the realm."

Lucas looks doubtful. "Maybe. I'll take it just in case. My senses aren't quite as good as yours, but it's worth a try." He takes the plastic bag containing the shirt and tucks it into his own back pocket.

The other witches and Taylor depart, leaving us to deal with my grandfather alone as a family. My mother snuggles into my father's side, and they whisper quietly to one another as I sink back into the couch, blowing out a huge breath.

"Are you okay?" Lucas asks, sitting down next to me and taking my hand in his.

I shake my head. "Not really."

"Come here." He puts his arm around me and pulls me into his side, and I let him. Closing my eyes, I soak in all the strength I can feel inside him, selfishly taking some of it for myself and leaning on someone for once in my life.

"I knew you would be a whore just like your slut mother before you." Grandfather's accented crackly voice breaks through the silence, but I ignore it, not ready to acknowledge his toxicity.

CHAPTER
Eleven

Lucas

I feel Tia stiffen under my arms at the venom in Mr. Lee's words, but she doesn't move, and she doesn't open her eyes, so I stay where I am, offering her all the support and comfort I can.

"Hello, Chen." My king's voice is low, but I hear the violence in those two little words.

Mr. Lee's eyes widen with shock, and he turns his head. "You," he hisses, his skin paling. "Get your filthy hands off my daughter."

"Oh, Chen, you have more things to worry about other than my hands being on your daughter. You tried to kill me. Thankfully, nobody told you how to really kill a vampire."

My grandfather interrupts him. "Oh, I knew, but that useless Silvan wasn't able to get his hands on that special wood for me. Otherwise, you'd be nothing but ash in my hardwood floor's cracks." Grandfather cackles evilly. "All of you would be. I won't have this family name tainted by vamp blood. I'd rather it die out than have any Lees with vampire blood."

"We aren't Lees. Tia and I are Blackwoods, and as far as I'm concerned, you can burn in hell," my mother says, her head held high.

"We will return to the vampire realm for the execution. My people will want to see the one responsible for my absence. I am going to have to talk to my sons and explain everything as well. Which of them is king?"

My mother and father turn their backs on my grandfather, not willing to give him any more attention, which infuriates him. He starts to spew more obscenities, but my mom just waves her hand, and he's instantly gagged.

She smiles, rubbing her palm with her other hand. "It is so good to have access to my power again."

My dad takes both hands and kisses them, and I can see their love is true and real, and for the first time, I feel hopeful.

"All three of them have been sharing the position equally, sir, and they have been doing a wonderful job. The vampire realm is thriving, though we just discovered another blood farm plot right before coming out here. They are stealing humans now that they have a witch to operate the portal," I explain from my position on the couch, not removing my arm from Tia's shoulders.

His eyes narrow, and he starts to open his mouth, but Fiona pinches and hushes him. He stares down at her in shock, not used to being put in his place, before he chuckles sheepishly. Fiona is going to be good for our king. She's obviously not afraid to argue with him.

"Right then, I guess now is as good a time as any for us to return. We will have that problem sorted out in no time, and then I can enjoy being with my wife and daughter. I can't wait to introduce you to my sons."

"Me neither," I say, but it's for a completely different reason. I stand up and offer Tia my hand, deciding to make sure she's okay with the plan. Nobody has really stopped to ask her opinion, and all of this is probably a lot, considering she just arrived to the island. Discovering your grandfather is an evil puppeteer who killed your grandmother and kept your mother in a puppet-like state for your entire lifetime is a lot to take in. Add that to a long-lost vampire father and the fact that you're three quarters vampire and only one quarter witch, and it's enough to cause any sane person to scream.

"Are you okay with this?" I ask her, and she shrugs as she takes my hand, allowing me to help her stand.

"Please tell me the vampire realm has tequila, because if not, we are going to be taking that bottle over there with us, and I plan to get plastered tonight. Just saying."

Like I thought, it is too much, and Tia seems to be hanging on by a thread. "Hey, look at me," I order, and she looks up at me with those beautiful eyes. I feel my heart clench in my chest. She looks like she's floating untethered on a breeze and desperately needs someone to reach out and give her some stability. "You can do this. I will help you every step of the way. I promise I will not leave your side until you feel like you can stand on your own two feet."

I hear Fiona sigh and Jarlen clear his throat, but I ignore them. I want Tia to know that I will put her well-being first, even if it annoys my king.

Her eyes fill with tears, and the strong, closed off woman I met this morning melts away before my eyes and is replaced by an insecure, shellshocked little girl. It triggers every one of my protective instincts, and I groan as she throws herself at me, wrapping her arms around my waist and burrowing into my chest.

"Thank you," she sobs, and the break I'd been expecting finally happens. She has nothing to be ashamed of as I hold her shaking body, and she lets all of her emotions out. Anyone would be doing the same thing in her place.

"Oh, sweetie." Fiona wrings her hands and bites her bottom lip as she watches her daughter fall apart. The two of them have so much between them that although I can see Fiona wants to help, it's going to take Tia a little while to get used to actually relying on her mother. For the first twenty-five years of her life, she couldn't, and although it wasn't Fiona's fault, that's not going to change instantly. They are going to have to get to know each other just like Tia and Jarlen are going to. It must be easier for her to sob on me, a stranger with no history but a strong attraction, than the absent parents she always wished for.

"I hate this." Jarlen picks up a knickknack and throws it across the room. It smashes against the wall above the fireplace before the shattered pieces drop to the ground. "You." He whirls on Mr. Lee. "You did this to us. I will see that you suffer a thousand deaths for your hand in this."

Over the top of Tia's head, I see Chen grinning at Jarlen without any remorse in his eyes.

"This is just the beginning. For so long, the witch race has been run by weak, emotional women. That is about to change, and us men will rise to the top and take control of everything we should have been in charge of from the start. Then we will see that the other inferior races are destroyed, and the portal is closed off so that we can't be influenced by abominations."

"Holy shit," Fiona mutters as Tia's sobs start to ease off. "He's fucking nuts." I can't help but think she's right, but where would he get these ideas from? All covens are matriarchal. Men still play a big role and are cherished, but a council of women usually leads each coven.

"Whether or not what he says is true, there is obviously some scheme at play. Are they all connected, or did they just have similar goals and decide to band together to help one another?" I stroke my hand over Tia's hair, trying to give her as much comfort as I can while attempting to keep up with the conversation. "I think we should return to the vampire realm and shut down the blood farm first. That is the most pressing issue, aside from the return of our king, of course. Then we need to assess the fae's involvement with all of this. I can reach out to Antoinette and see what she knows. For all we know, the dark entity was lying. They do like to stir up trouble."

"That is a solid plan, Lucas. I knew you would be an

asset to my sons. I am thankful they have had you to advise them while I've been gone."

Tia pulls back and looks at me, wide-eyed at her father's declaration. She seems to have cried everything out, and now she just looks slightly panicked at her father's words like she's suddenly worried about me. That hits me right in the chest. It's been a long time since I had someone worry about me, and it feels nice.

I rub her back reassuringly, and she stays where she is. I can practically feel how grateful she is that we let her have her very public breakdown but aren't drawing attention to it. It's going to take Tia a little while to adjust to being able to feel again. But I won't accept anything less, and I'm pretty sure her parents won't either. We just have to be patient.

"Before I fill you in on everything, shall we get moving? I would feel so much better if we could get you back to the right realm. No offense." I bow my head to Fiona, and she quickly shakes her own.

"Of course, I don't blame you one bit. Being here doesn't feel safe, and I will never return. My place is with Jarlen now, and his place is in the vampire realm. I would burn this place to the ground, but Tia may like it one day, so for now, we will close it up."

Tia sighs heavily and pulls away from me. I'm reluctant to let her go, not knowing if or when I'll ever have her back in my arms again, but I won't push my agenda just yet.

"I doubt I'll ever want to live in this house," she replies. "I wasn't even planning on staying on the island. I have a life to return to."

Those are the words that I have been dreading, and I

can tell by the looks on her parents' faces that they are shocked too. I want to snatch her up and take her to my place in the vampire realm and never let her go.

She holds her hands up before any of us can argue with her. "I now know that isn't going to be possible with me being part vampire, but whether I want to live in the vampire realm or here is yet to be determined, so leave it for now. We can deal with it later."

"Your vampire awakening will take a week, and if I use my pull, I can probably get you an appointment as soon as we return. Once you are through that, we can reassess. Does that sound acceptable to you?" Jarlen asks Tia, and it's all I can do not to growl my displeasure at the thought of her getting an awakening appointment with one of the blood consorts.

"Well, actually, I would like Lucas to see me through my awakening."

Jarlen's eyes narrow, and his head swivels to look at me. I blank my face, not outwardly wanting to challenge my king but not backing down either. I want him to know that I'm serious. I also desperately want to roar my pleasure to the sky and pound on my chest in response to her words, but I'm almost certain I would end up with my own stake in my chest before I'm shoved into some random closet. I can already tell that despite his quiet calm demeanor, he is going to be a fearsome father for Tia. She is really in for a rude shock since she has never experienced that before except from Pru and the coven.

Fiona looks between the two of us and smiles widely. "That sounds wonderful. I'm sure Lucas will be a wonderful blood consort." Jarlen goes to say something, but Fiona just elbows him, and a breath whooshes out as he doubles over. "Don't you think, darling?" We can all hear the threat behind the question, and Tia puts a hand over her mouth to smother her giggle. Hearing that sound again lifts a heavy weight off my shoulders. I think we're going to be okay.

Jarlen coughs, and Fiona thumps him on the back. "Yes, dear, I'm sure you are right," he replies, though I can see the warning in his eyes when he looks at me. The meaning is clear—hurt Tia, and I will pay. I hope he sees the determination and promise in my own eyes, because that will never happen.

"Okay then, that's settled, so let's get out of here. My father's car keys are in the dish by the door. If you two get them and bring the car around, Jarlen can help me bring my father out to the car," Fiona suggests, taking charge, and Tia grabs my hand and drags me away from her parents.

I can feel her father's stare between my shoulder blades, but I stand proud, pleased as can be at Tia's declaration. It's only a matter of time before I get my hands and fangs on this woman, and I can't wait.

Chen's car is an old station wagon, and Jarlen and Fiona lift him into the back before closing it and hopping into the back seat. They snuggle together as I make our way back toward the manor.

"So what did you want to fill me in on? Something

about advising my sons?" Jarlen asks, and I know I have to tell him what has been going on since he left.

"Ah, actually, I left the vampire realm three years ago, and I've been the mayor here on Morbank Island for the last two," I tell him, and he frowns, leaning forward.

"Why is that?" he asks, and I stammer over my words. I'm not entirely sure how to explain everything to him. "Last I knew, you were on track to take over as ambassador to the fae realm for your father. What happened?"

"You see, I wasn't interested in that position at all. My father was the one who wanted that to happen." The king frowns but doesn't interrupt me. "My sister is the ambassador to the fae."

That brings a smile to his lips. "Antoinette? Such a lovely girl. I saw the crush she had on my boys. I was hoping that something may have come from that, and one or all of them might have come to their senses and noticed what was right in front of them, but I guess they didn't if she is in the fae realm."

"No, they didn't," I grind out between gritted teeth, remembering their treatment of her. Oh, they weren't nasty or anything, just blind and careless with her emotions without even knowing.

"So you were angry with them?" he presses, and I shrug.

"Somewhat, but my dad disowned me when I declined to become ambassador, and my mother didn't do anything to stop him. I felt like a change in scenery would be better than sticking around and listening to him constantly criticize me."

"Hmm. I'm sorry to hear that, Lucas. I never would have thought your father was capable of such behavior. It seems a lot has changed in my absence."

"Yes and no. I haven't been back for a while, so I can't tell you for sure, but Regan and Tatiana both said that everything seemed to be fine in the vampire realm when they visited a couple of weeks ago."

"And why was that?" he asks, and so I spend the rest of the trip back to the manor explaining about the realm tours and what has been happening here on Morbank Island. Thankfully, he seems to fully approve of them and won't put a kink in Regan's plans.

"It's about time the realms were opened up and travel between them was more frequent," he says as I park Mr. Lee's old station wagon in front of the manor. The valet comes running out, and his eyes just about pop out of his head when Jarlen and Fiona drag Mr. Lee out of the back.

I toss him the keys.

"I'm not sure when we'll be back, so please let Regan know he can have the car towed if it gets in the way," Fiona tells the boy who is still speechless, and then she floats Mr. Lee up the steps.

"Ah, sure," he stutters, his eyes not leaving the spectacle, and Tia giggles. It's a relief to hear it, because she was quiet while I explained everything to her father.

"Are you ready for this?" I ask her once Jarlen and Fiona have entered the manor. A shout from inside tells us that someone is obviously at the desk.

"No, but I guess there's nothing I can do to delay it." She gnaws on her lip, and all I want to do is soothe them with my own, but that will have to wait. I'll get my hands and fangs on this delicious woman soon enough.

"Come on. Mac has to come up and get us. I don't want him to have to do two trips. Everything will be fine, I promise. I'll be with you every step of the way."

CHAPTER
Twelve

Ruby

I'm all kinds of blown away by today's revelations. When we came out here to confront Tia's crusty old grandpa, I never would have thought we'd find a missing vampire king, and I don't think I'm the only one. When we step out of the cottage, I shiver as a rush of cool air blows around us, and it's still warmer than the atmosphere inside.

"Does anyone else feel exhausted?" I ask as I follow my mother and Laura down the steps and out into the barren front yard. I can hear Tatiana and my brother arguing quietly behind me, but I don't have the energy to be nosy.

Taylor raises his hand. "I am, and I didn't even help with that spell. I kind of wished I hadn't gotten out of bed today," he grumbles, and my mom smiles at him affectionately.

"Doesn't mean it wouldn't have all been here for you tomorrow," she says, and he grimaces.

"Banishing that entity took a good deal of power. I don't know about you, but I could use some replenishing before we confront William." Laura looks a little paler than she was earlier, and Mom nods.

"Let's go to Happy Herbs. We can talk to Minerva about what happened today, and she will have some vitality potions on hand which should help us regain energy. We can also talk to her about providing selenite for all of our supernaturals."

"What do you want to do about William? Do you want him contained in the special cell at the sheriff's office?" Taylor asks.

"My concern is that he is not smart enough to be acting on his own, and if we contain him there, someone will spring him. We have the supernatural containment cells beneath the manor, and I think that would be the best place for him."

Regan breaks off from his argument with Tatiana and steps forward.

"Do you think Susan has anything to do with any of this?" I ask him, trying to gauge his feelings on everything we've learned.

He shrugs. "I have no idea. I haven't heard from her since she left. Even when I filed for divorce and full custody of the children, she was a no-show in court. She could be. She wasn't happy that she wasn't one of the ten selected to be a part of the next council."

I scoff. "Why would she be? Our ten families have been the council representatives for hundreds of years. Her family only applied to join the coven when we were in grade school. I remember when she and William first arrived. William told me I was a gross girl and pushed me into a puddle, and Susan laughed."

"She was nasty from day one. I have no idea what you saw in her, Regan." Tatiana nudges my brother, who blushes and mumbles something.

"I'm sorry, what was that?" I ask him, not sure I heard him right.

"She was a drunken one-night stand, and the twins were the result. I thought I had to do the right thing and marry her."

"Seriously?" my mother screeches. "Regan, you're an idiot. We never would have expected you to marry her. We thought you loved her. She certainly seemed like she loved you."

"She told me if I didn't pretend in public, she would take the children and disappear, and I would never see them again."

"That bitch just gets nastier and nastier. Why put you through all that if she was going to bail after the birth anyway?" I ask, and he shakes his head.

"I have no idea, but apart from the day the twins were born, it was the happiest day of my life."

"I think it's time we tracked Susan down, don't you?" Mom suggests, and his eyes widen with panic.

"No. No way. What if she wants the kids?"

"Baby, you have full custody. She can't do anything with them." Tatiana rubs her hand up and down my brother's back soothingly, and I see the tension drain out of him. They are so cute together.

"Fine, but let's deal with William first. She may turn back up when he has to stand before the coven council."

"He won't just have to stand before the coven council. He will have to stand before the supernatural council. He's been using the portal for his own personal gain and will have to answer for his crimes," my mother announces, and I feel a shiver shudder down my spine. Shit, that's not good. It's going to gain more of the council's attention, and we're already on shaky ground because of the portal fluctuations.

"Well, that's certainly not good," I grumble, and nobody disagrees with me.

Tatiana looks back at the cottage and bites her lip. I can tell she's hiding something.

"Alright, what is eating at you? You've been fidgeting since we walked out of there," I remark, and she looks at my brother who sighs.

"Not here. We'll tell you everything at Happy Herbs."

"Well, let's go then," I demand.

Taylor sighs heavily. "Is this something I need to know about? Something that directly affects the coven or the case I'm currently working?" he asks.

"No. I don't think it's anything you need to know for now. It has nothing to do with the blood farms and the missing human anyway," Regan assures him, and Taylor nods.

"Well, I will leave you be then. I have to go back and write a report on what we found. Pru, if you wouldn't mind, please move my clothes to my office so I have something to wear when I get back there."

"Of course, Taylor. If you could hold off on telling them that their friend has been trafficked, I would appreciate it. I'm not sure the supernatural council would want that getting out. It will cause nothing but widespread panic amongst the human population, and if we can ask the vampires to implant new memories or just wipe the old ones, well, that would be better for everyone involved," my mom suggests.

"I agree. I will tell them we have tracked her to the vampire realm and that we have someone going there to find what happened after that. I'll make it sound like she got caught up in a whirlwind affair with the vampire, and hopefully that will ease their concerns somewhat. I hope it doesn't take Lucas and Jarlen too long to find her."

Taylor strips to his underwear and shifts. My mother waves a hand and transfers his belongings to the sheriff's office, and then we all teleport to Happy Herbs.

My mother pushes the door open, and we all follow her inside. The store smells like heaven. All the herbs and spices a witch could ever need are mixed together in a cornucopia of scents. Goosebumps rise on my skin in response, and pride rolls through me for my witch heritage and how wonderful it is to have the number one apothecary supply store in the country here in our little town.

"I won't be a moment," a cheerful voice calls from somewhere deep inside the store in response to the bell that rang when we entered.

Instead of wandering the aisles like I'm dying to do so I can see any new products Minerva may have put out since I was in here last, I follow my mother to the back of the store where the register and work rooms are. Much like my candy store used to be, the work room is at the back of the store. It's where Minerva and her team create all their wonderful products and bag up raw ingredients to send across the country to people needing them for their own spells and rituals.

A table of raw and polished stones and crystals catches my eye, and I look for the familiar white of selenite. Seeing it, I gather up the whole bowl and take it with me. There's no time like the present to get started on outfitting our coven members with it. We may have to bring Marie Payne in as well. She can craft us all jewelry pieces with the stone in it, something that can be worn so we can all see that each of us are dark entity free.

When I get to the back, I place the bowl down on the counter. "Oh, good thinking," Mom says, but loud arguing from inside the workroom draws our attention. There are some colorful plastic strips hanging in the doorway between the two areas, but they do nothing to block out sound.

"No, Meadow. I don't think it's a good idea for us to be adding marijuana to our catalog. If that's what you want to do with your life, then I can't stop you, but I doubt there is much of a demand for weed to make it worth us converting some of our greenhouses for you to grow it."

"Ah, shit. Meadow said her mom would be stubborn about growing weed," Tatiana mutters. "She was as reluctant to return as Tatiana, but she did so for the sake of the coven. If Minerva doesn't change her mind, she won't stay once we have rid the island of the malicious spell either."

"Why is Minerva being stubborn? She has certainly enjoyed indulging with us after our full moon parties."

Laura sounds surprised, and from the look on Mom's face, she is too.

"Meadow says it's a matter of pride. They are the foremost apothecary supplier to most of the country's covens. She said adding weed to her inventory would be playing to the masses."

"But, Mom," Meadow argues, "there is so much more to it than just getting high. It helps so many people with treatments that modern medicine some-times can't help with—cancer patients, people with MS and Parkinson's, even anxiety and ADHD. It's not all about getting stoned, though that is very lucrative too. Here, these are the figures for just one of the High Hopes dispensaries. This is their weekly profit."

It's quiet for a moment. "Goddess above, that is profit?" I can tell by Minerva's voice that she is impressed.

"It sure is." Meadow's reply sounds smug. "And with our magic, we can generate this kind of income within weeks."

"Fine, I'll talk with your father tonight and see which greenhouse you can have. Just one to start with, okay? Now I have customers. Write up a plan to present to your dad after work this evening. He will want to see those numbers too."

We hear Meadow squeal with excitement, and I feel the tension drain out of me. Hopefully this will mean she's not in such a hurry to leave again if she has some-thing to keep her occupied.

Minerva sweeps through the plastic divider, the strips falling back into place in her wake. She has a smile plastered on her face, but when she sees it's just us, it drops, and she rolls her eyes in exasperation. "I don't know how I let that girl talk me into things."

"It's because we made mistakes, and now we need to own up to them. I have thought about all the things I could say to Estrella when she gets back, but the one that sticks out the most is 'I'm sorry.'" Laura leans over and pats Minerva on the hand. "Just be happy she's here."

"Oh, I am, I really am," she assures her, and I feel guilty.

"Right. As soon as we are done here, I'll do a locator spell for the rest of the girls, and I won't come back until they are all convinced to return," I promise, no longer willing to wait for the spell to work on my friends like it did me. They've all proven they need a shove. I wonder if it's because Fiona wasn't at full power and was being used by Mr. Lee. The ten of them should have had enough juice to bring us all home, but it isn't working out that way.

"What can I do for you? I must say I'm a little surprised to see you all together, though I'm not upset that you came to visit. We don't see each other enough anymore. Meadow, get out here. Some of the coven members are visiting."

Within moments, my beautiful friend comes through the door. I saw her when we went up to the farm she'd been working at to get her, but I'd left her and Tatiana to return on their own when I'd gone to find Tia. She looks gorgeous, as usual. Her long, blond hair hangs down her back in beachy waves, and her various piercings all sparkle with gems. She's wearing a maxi dress with a large, boyfriend style cardigan over the top. She smiles widely and gives Mom, Laura, and Regan big hugs and kisses them on the cheek.

"Hey, bitches!" She hip bumps me and Tati, the dozens of bracelets on her wrist jingling loudly. Now that she's around this side, I can see she has on leggings and Converse under her maxi dress, well-adjusted to the colder weather of Morbank. I was worried she changed into the quintessential Cali girl and was going to freeze, but I should have known better. Meadow is like a chameleon, and she's able to adapt to whatever environment she finds herself in.

Mom tells Meadow and Minerva exactly what happened over the last couple of hours. Shit, I can't believe Tatiana and I arrived back only this morning. So much has happened.

"Now what were the two of you whispering about?" I ask Tatiana and my brother once the two Crowe women express their disgust and outrage over both Mr. Lee and William.

"When we were in the fae realm, it was pretty clear that all is not completely right," Regan hedges, and Tatiana rolls her eyes, huffing.

"The crown prince is a giant douche, and we think he is holding the vampire ambassador captive, or at least denying her blood so she will feed off of him. He is a vamp bite junky, not to mention other things."

"So it's no real surprise to hear that he is involved with Chen and whatever the vampires have planned."

Regan shrugs. "No, not really, but I am reluctant to say anything in case politics between the two of them blow up and ruin our realm tours. Morbank is finally getting back on track, and I would have to cancel them before they even really got off the ground."

"Regan," my mother scolds, and he blushes, but I do feel sorry for the guy because he has worked so hard for this.

"I know, but we did hint to Cole that all was not right. I'm hoping he did something about it. Now that the manor is mostly restaffed, though, I thought both Tatiana and I could accompany the groups to start with and make sure that everything is okay. Just give me a few weeks, and we can also assess if what they told us is true. It may not be, and I'd like to be sure before I start pointing fingers at the crown prince of the fae. Could you imagine the fall out if the dark entity was lying?"

I watch my mother mull it over in her head.

"He's not wrong, that would be a disaster," Minerva agrees.

"But you should have seen the vampire ambassador. She looked terrible," Tatiana argues, and my mother sighs.

"I'm sure now that Jarlen has returned, he will stay on top of things, but if you are still worried for her after the first couple of tours, I will speak to the king myself. By then, the tours should be well established. We have to worry about our coven first and foremost, and at the moment, those tours are a big deal to us and our ability to look after the portal." Mom uses her leader of the coven voice, and while it's obvious Tatiana wants to argue, she doesn't, especially with Laura and Minerva nodding their agreement.

"Right, so I need to go speak to William. I'd appreciate it if you two would accompany me," she tells the two older women who both quickly agree. "Are you three coming?" she asks Tatiana, Regan, and me. Meadow is going to look after the shop for Minerva.

"Yes, of course." My brother scowls. "I want to confront that asshole."

She looks at me. "Ah, no, Tatiana and I will stay here. You don't need us, and if there are too many of us, it might make it easier for him to get away."

Tatiana goes to argue, but I subtly kick her, and she shuts up.

"Okay, we'll see you back at the manor later then... probably." My mom is eyeing me suspiciously, but what she has to do is too important for her to get distracted, so she sweeps out, followed by my brother and her fellow coven members. They have to teleport from the front of the building because, like the manor, the business is protected from direct teleportation.

As soon as they leave, Meadow waves a hand, locking the front door and putting up the "out for lunch" sign. She then conjures up a bag of joints, pulls one out, and lights it. "God, I thought that woman was never going to get off my back." She chuckles. "While it was nice to see them, staying at home is not going to work. I need to move out."

"Why don't you move into the apartment above?" I ask, pointing to the ceiling, and she wrinkles up her nose.

"Because Cullen got in there first. He offered to let me move in, but he has unsociable hours from working at the Buttered Biscuit, and they probably won't get any better now that he's agreed to do the manor's desserts and pastries too."

"Regan was thrilled when Cullen came to him and asked for the position of dessert and pastry chef. We thought he was happy at the Buttered Biscuit," Tatiana replies, and Meadow shrugs.

"You know my brother. He doesn't like to keep still, and while he enjoys working at the Buttered Biscuit, I think he was ready to be in charge as opposed to the person who took instructions from the owners, and Lucille and Phillip are thrilled for him. They know he's ready to do more."

"So we need to find you somewhere to live. You are welcome to come and stay with me at my cottage if you want," I offer, and she looks interested, but Tatiana shakes her head.

"Don't do it. Ruby has a loft bedroom, and my brother is there a lot."

Meadow's eyes widen comically, and she fake gags.

"No thanks. I don't need intimate knowledge of your and Maddox's sex life."

"But weren't you talking about moving in together? That would mean my brother's apartment will be up for rent," Tatiana suggests.

"Oh yes, perfect." I clap my hands. "I'll talk to him about it tonight."

Tatiana puts her hands on her hips and glares at me. "Now what are you scheming?"

"Who, me?" I ask innocently, putting a hand to my chest and fluttering my eyelashes.

"Yes. Don't forget what happened last time you had a grand plan. We ended up with three Regans."

Jesus, you make one itty bitty mistake and your friends never let you forget it. "No, I just wondered if there was a spell we could give the vampire ambassador to help with her protection. Maybe something that could make her bite painful instead of pleasurable. That would at least ensure her safety until the realm tours are established."

I've barely finished my sentence before Tatiana throws her arms around me and smacks a huge kiss on my cheek. "You really are the best," she says as she pulls away, and I scoff.

"Please, bitch, you just doubted me. Make up your mind." I push her away, although I'm secretly preening.

"Where will we find a spell like that?" Meadow's cloud of weed smoke is starting to overpower the rest of the scents in the shop.

I snatch the joint out of her hand and put it to my lips. "Well, from Nana of course," I tell them. "But I'm going to need a couple of hits from this in case Nana and Grandpa are getting jiggy with it when I scry her."

CHAPTER
Thirteen

Tia

I've never been down in the portal room, and to say Mac was speechless to see my father was an understatement. He stuttered a few times before giving up and bowing.

My dad just slapped him on the back. "Good to see you again, Mac. It's been a while. You got old." My dad chuckles, and Mac stares at him in disbelief before joining in and turning to my mom.

"I might have, but you certainly didn't. Wow, Fiona, you look just like you did twenty-five years ago." He gives my mom a hug and kiss on the cheek. "Regan didn't fill me in on what was happening, he just said that the king had been found and an immediate portal to the vampire realm was needed. He also muttered something about your dad. Can't say I'm surprised." He looks between us, giving my bound grandfather an icy glare before his gaze lands on Lucas.

"We don't have time to stop and tell you the whole story, but Regan will be back later, and I'm sure he will fill you in."

Mac nods as the elevator stops in the portal room, and we step out. "I've sent a message through to the vamp realm, but I haven't had a response yet," he tells us, and my father frowns.

"Is that normal?" he asks, and Mac nods.

"Yes, the portal desk there isn't manned permanently like ours is. They usually get back to us within a couple of hours. It's never been urgent before. I'm afraid you will probably be met with armed guards on the other side. The alarm will sound, and they will come running because of the unscheduled portal opening."

"One of the guards or the person who mans the portal must be in on the trafficking if there is an alarm, otherwise the whole palace would know about the unscheduled portal openings," my father says to Lucas. "I guess that's how they managed to get all the humans through. We will have to fix that immediately." My dad sounds annoyed.

"Especially if it's late at night. You know what vampires are like, and the palace is usually a massive orgy after dinner."

Holy shit. My mother and I exchange a glance, and she raises an unimpressed eyebrow. I can guarantee things are going to change if public sexual displays are a thing. My mom will have that behind closed doors faster than you can say prude.

"Don't be too hard on your sons. A faction, who I'm now guessing is in on the whole trafficking thing, pressured them to have it unmanned. They said it cost the realm to have someone sit there all the time when it's hardly used. They weren't wrong. Portal use has died down in the last couple of years. After you went missing, accusations were flying all over the place, and interspecies relations were at an all-time low. We are hopeful that with Regan's new tour concept, we may be able to improve travel to all realms," he says. "Well, good luck with finding the missing humans. Hopefully they are still alive, or that is going to become a whole other problem for the supernatural community." Mac leaves us and goes into the operating room.

I finally turn my attention to the portal, surprised by what I see. I guess I let human television influence my mind, because I expected to see a round metal ring with funny symbols on it. Instead, it's a huge piece of wood shaped like a doorway with runes carved into it. It's wide and high enough to drive a truck through, and it sits at one end of the room with the waiting area in front of it.

We see Mac push a few buttons on the console, activating the portal, and goosebumps erupt across my skin as I feel magic tingle in the air. Suddenly, a cloudy mist appears within the frame. "Alright, let's go. Fiona, my love, take my hand. It can be a bit disorienting when you first go through it. Lucas, can you please help Tia?"

A rush of excitement flows through my body as Lucas takes my hand in his. Holy crap, this is it. We're going to the vampire realm, we are going to lift whatever spell is still on me, and I'm going to have my vampire awakening. I kind of feel like I need to stop and take a breath, but at the same time, I want to say screw it and rush headfirst into this. I've always been so cautious all my life. It stems from having to tiptoe around my grandfather, never wanting to incur his wrath. I was even methodical and careful with all of my pyrotechnic training, since you can never be too careful around explosives. For once, I just want to be like a bull in a china shop and barge right through life.

Lucas squeezes my hand, and the two of us lead the way through the portal, followed by my parents. The mist is cold on my bare arms, and my breath puffs out in front of me, but we only take a few steps before we emerge on the other side.

Sure enough, there is a loud alarm signaling our arrival, as well as some red flashing lights. The room, which looks like it could be a castle if the stone blocks tell me anything, is flooded with bright light, and I squint against the glare. In a flash, the area is filled with vampire guards all pointing various weapons at us. Some have guns, and others hold medieval weaponry.

One steps forward, frowning heavily. He's not wearing a uniform like the others, and he has dark hair and piercing blue eyes. He also has the same other-worldly look that Lucas has. "Lucas? What is the meaning of this? You weren't scheduled for a portal."

"Wow, Cole, is that how you greet one of your oldest friends now?" You can't miss the sarcasm in Lucas's voice.

"Why are you here? You said it would be a cold day in hell before you voluntarily came back for a visit." Cole sounds disgruntled, and I'm guessing he was not happy about that.

"What can I say, I come bearing gifts." Lucas smirks.

Cole's glare drops, and he looks at me with interest. "Oh, what? Not the pretty little thing next to you? While she's lovely, you know I don't have time for flings, what with keeping the kings in line and all."

Lucas growls. "No, asshole, Tia is with me." He pushes me behind him, and I smother the grin that wants to form at his possessiveness.

Cole raises an eyebrow at that statement.

"That would be me." My father gently pushes past Lucas and me, and Cole just about swallows his tongue. He stammers, and all the guards around him drop to one knee and bow their heads.

"Uncle? But how... and where... and what?" Cole mutters, looking between the two vampire men. King Jarlen holds out his arms and walks over to embrace his stunned nephew.

"Cole, my boy, you are looking well." They embrace, and I hear them exchange some emotion-filled words. The guards stay motionless on the floor, but out of the corner of my eye, I see one of them watching with panic on his face.

"It's a long story. I don't want to really tell it too often, so let's find the boys, and I can tell everyone at once."

"Yes, of course, uncle, right away. Marcus!" The guard I was watching jumps to his feet. "Go tell the kings that a very important visitor has arrived. Have them meet us in their private meeting room behind the throne room. Go straight there and tell no one else about this just yet."

The man does as Cole asks and races away.

"Rise, my people. It is good to see you still protect

our kingdom so well." My father is gracious, but as the guards get to their feet, I see him eyeing them all carefully. "I recognize a few faces from before. It is lovely to see you again, and I look forward to meeting any of the new ones. Now be at ease, but please keep my return to yourselves until I can speak to my family."

The guards all bow their heads, and some of them express thanks to the vampire goddess for his return before they all leave.

Now that the immediate threat has gone, I shiver from how cold it is in the room, and my father must notice, because he reaches out to squeeze my hand. "Oh, my poor girl. The palace is cold apart from the receiving rooms. Come, we will get you something warm to put on. Until your awakening, you will feel the cold, but after that, temperature change won't bother you so much."

"How are we going to get to the receiving room without being seen? If we go the public way, news of your return will spread through the realm like wildfire before we even get there," Lucas asks, putting his arm around my shoulders to help ward off the chill, and my father nods his thanks to him before dropping his hand. Lucas's body heat is delicious, and I find myself snuggling into him.

Cole is watching us carefully, and he grins widely at what he sees. "Well, my friend, if you stuck around and took one of the positions your friends and kings offered you, then you would know all the secrets too."

He walks over to a wall that has an old-fashioned sconce on it. It's unlit, and he reaches up and pulls it down. Sure enough—completely cliched but also completely awesome—a part of the wall opens, revealing a hidden passageway. He grabs a torch from the wall inside and looks at Fiona.

"Ms. Blackwell, if you don't mind." He holds out the torch, and my mom waves her hand, and it flares to life. "I must say you are looking different than the last time I saw you on Morbank." Cole is exceedingly polite, but he can't hide his curiosity, and it turns to incredulity when she waves my bound grandfather forward. "Holy shit, is that Mr. Lee?"

"Yes. I'm afraid my father has committed grievous crimes against the vampire nation and must now pay for those crimes." Fiona glares at her father.

"Not to mention the crimes he committed against his own flesh and blood," my father adds, and if glares could kill, my grandfather would be ashes on the floor from the strength of Jarlen's gaze. I think he's more upset about what grandfather did to Mom and me than what he did to him.

Cole leads the way through the inside walls of what Lucas explains is the palace and the main residence for the king, his family, and the numerous advisors and people of the court—lords and ladies and that sort of thing. It seems that the vampire realm has a feudal system in place, as does the fae realm, and they both have a king that oversees it all. The king has advisors and can bestow land and titles as he sees fit. The shifter realm is run by a council system, with each shifter species having an alpha of alphas that represents them.

Normally, one of my father's sons—my brothers, wow—would have inherited the role of king, but because they are triplets and refused to admit who was born first, the vampire people had no choice but to accept all three as joint rulers. I think it's a great idea. There are three of them, which means someone always has the deciding vote.

"Here we are." Cole pulls down on a lever on the inside of the wall, and another door opens. I squint against the bright light, my eyes having adjusted to the darkness and the dull glare of the torch. Cole steps out first, and I follow him to find three men already waiting for us.

"Cole, Marcus said you wanted to see us. What are you using the tunnels for?" one of the men demands. He's sprawled on a comfy sofa, and like Cole, he has piercing blue eyes and that ethereal look about him, but his dark hair is long and tied back in a ponytail at the nape of his neck. He frowns in my direction. "You didn't bring us women, did you? How many times do I have to tell you that we are sick of having women paraded in front of us like they are prized cows?"

"No." Lucas follows me out, glaring at the three men. "Tia is with me, Jacob." Lucas all but brands a claimed stamp on my forehead. "Though I think you're going to regret your words in a moment." He chuckles and drags me closer to the fire, where he helps me into a seat. The other two men are obviously Jacob's brothers, and although they look alike, they are easy to tell apart. I think that's only because of their different hair styles though. If they all had the same one, I think it would be hard. One has a short military style haircut, and the other has shaved sides with longer locks on top, and it's styled artfully back off his face.

I see the exact moment they catch sight of their

father. All the color drains away from their faces, and their bodies go on alert.

"Dad?" The one with the military haircut steps away from the bar. "Oh my god, Dad!" he shouts and flashes to his father's side, throwing his arms around him.

"Hello, Jeremiah. God, I missed you all," my father mumbles into his son's shoulder as they hug fiercely. Jacob joins them, and it turns into a three-way hug as my mom emerges from the tunnel, followed by my grandfather who is still immobile but being moved by a locomotion spell.

"But how?" The last one hasn't moved from his spot on the other side of the bar. His eyes are wide as he looks between us.

"Oh, Jett, come over here and hug me, and then I'll tell you all." Jarlen holds out an arm, and his final son joins them. Tears of joy flow down all their faces, and I feel a lump form in my throat. Wow, the king really loves his sons and vice versa. That gives me hope that maybe, just maybe, there might be room for me in this family too.

My mom waves my grandfather into the corner, making him face the wall. It's kind of savage, because it will drive my grandfather nuts not being able to see what is happening. She then joins me on the sofa and grabs my hand, giving it a squeeze.

"Are you nervous?" I ask her, and she bites her lip and nods quickly, never taking her eyes off the men.

"Yes, very," she replies.

"Don't be. It's easy to see the king is besotted with you. His sons will be soon enough too. They will love you, I promise," Lucas tells my mother, and I snuggle into his side. He's so sweet, trying to reassure her.

"But how, Dad? Where have you been all this time?" Jett pulls back from the emotional family reunion, his gaze drifting to us. "Where did you find him, Lucas? Where have you been all this time? Why weren't you here?" His eyes narrow suspiciously on us. "Who are these women? Are they the reason you haven't been around? Found yourself a harem, have you?" His last words are harsh, and I hear Lucas snort with amusement.

"And what's with the old man in the corner?" Jacob retakes his seat on the sofa, but he's not as relaxed as he was before.

"Don't be like that, son. There is a legitimate reason why I wasn't here, and I'll get into that shortly, but first, I'd like you to meet my mate, Fiona, and your sister, Tia." The king turns and gestures for my mom to join him. My mom gets up and glides over to him, and he wraps an arm around her.

"Fiona, these are my boys, Jacob, Jett, and Jeremiah." He gestures to each of them in turn.

"It's lovely to finally meet you boys. I've been looking forward to this for a long time," my mother says carefully, and the boys are speechless. I can't stop the giggle that escapes. At the sound of my laughter, all three of them turn to look at me.

"And did you say sister?" Jeremiah asks, his eyes narrowing as he takes me in as I snuggle next to Lucas.

"Yes, come sit down. We will have drinks, and I'll explain."

CHAPTER
Fourteen

Lucas

For the next hour, Jarlen and Fiona tell his sons exactly what happened. When they learned of Mr. Lee's part in the whole plot, they had him carted off to the dungeons.

Cole threw himself at Jarlen's feet and begged for forgiveness when he found out his brother had a hand in all of this.

"Nonsense, my boy, get up. I know you are loyal, and his actions are not yours. I don't want to hear you talk like that at all." Jarlen is fierce in his reaction, and Cole climbs back to his feet, but I can tell by the set of his shoulders that he is still embarrassed and ashamed.

As expected, the guys were thrilled their dad found his mate, and they gave Fiona a warm reception. They were stunned to find out that they had a child together and she had basically been held captive her whole life. I watched with amusement as all three of them dropped to their knees in front of Tia and promised to painfully kill anyone who hurts her from here on out.

Tia thanked them politely, but they will have to prove it to her for her to believe them. Her only family let her down badly in the past, so she will need actions rather than words.

"Tia needs to go through her vampire awakening. We need to arrange it. Is there still a schedule, and are the rooms still used? We need to get her booked in," Jarlen says, and like one entity, they all pale slightly.

"Are you sure she needs to go through the awakening? Maybe once we break the pendant, her vampire traits will naturally rise," Jacob suggests, and I feel Tia stiffen in outrage.

But before she can say anything, the king frowns at his sons.

"You know that's not how it happens. What's wrong, boys? Why shouldn't you want your sister to go through her awakening?"

"Dad, you know what happens during an awakening," Jett hisses and squirms uncomfortably. "I don't like the idea of any of our blood consorts helping her with that."

"Well, it's lucky that Lucas has volunteered to help her through her awakening then, isn't it?" An amused smile spreads across my king's face, and he turns to look at me. "I couldn't think of a more capable and honorable vampire to help her. Right, boys?" He turns back to them, grinning.

All three of them are now glaring at me like I just

told them I was going to deflower their virgin sister. Oh, hang on, that's pretty much what I'm going to do.

"What the hell, man? You offered to help our sister through her awakening? What is this, some kind of payback for us ignoring your sister?"

My amusement fades as I feel Tia flinch like Jeremiah just struck her. I remove my arm from her shoulders and stand up, unable to stop the lethal growl that escapes my lips. "Because you were once my best friend, I am going to give you one chance to apologize for that bitch ass comment before I rip your fucking head off your shoulders."

"Well, isn't he right? You didn't like how we treated Nettie, and this is payback," Jacob sneers and takes a step forward. I take my own step, pressing my chest against his and refusing to back down despite him being my king.

"This has nothing to do with you at all, you self-involved asshole. How dare you belittle my attraction to Tia like that. I felt an instant connection to her the moment my eyes met hers, and that was long before I found out she was a vamp, let alone your sister, so back the fuck off, or I will make you."

"That's enough." Fiona's voice thunders through the room, and she waves her hand, freezing us all. "Don't you think Tia deserves a chance to speak?" She keeps us frozen as her daughter steps up, her own rage flashing in her eyes as those pretty fireworks cover her body. Her brothers' eyes widen in surprise, but Jarlen just looks smug and pleased.

"I'd like to say that the overprotectiveness is nice, but

it's really not. I've had to look out for myself for as long as I can remember." Both her parents flinch at this, though I'm almost certain she doesn't mean it as an attack. "I decide what I do with my body and whom I do it with. Lucas is right, there is something between us. I feel drawn to him like no man I've ever met before. His blood practically sang to me when he threw himself in front of my grandfather's attack to protect me. I also like what his bite did to me when I offered him my blood to repay him for shielding me. Lucas is my choice, and you can live with it or Mom can keep you frozen until it is done."

I feel a rush of heat flow through my body at Tia's claim and defense of her choice. I think she's my mate, because her blood tasted better than any I've had before, but without intimate contact, I won't know for sure. There is always a chance it's just good chemistry. If it is, I'm not sure how I'll recover. I desperately want her to be my mate. I want to spend the rest of my long life spoiling her and giving her the love and devotion she hasn't had for the last twenty-five years.

Jarlen chuckles, and although he has been reserved and giving her a chance to adjust to everything, this time he can't resist hugging her. "That's my girl. Stand up to your brothers. They need to be put in their place occasionally." He sounds so proud, and Fiona is beaming with delight. Tia hesitantly hugs him back, and by the time he pulls away, I can see she has melted into him, reveling in the contact from her father.

"Well, it's been a night for revelations. How about I show Lucas and Tia to some rooms, and tomorrow we can announce your return to the realm?" Cole, ever the peacemaker and the triplets' right-hand man, steps forward, breaking the tension.

Fiona waves her hand and unfreezes us. All three of them start to say something, but Jarlen doesn't let them.

"Silence. I don't want to hear another word from any of you. Do not ruin our reunion with petty arguments. Lucas is Tia's choice, and you need to respect that. I can only hope that when you choose your consorts or find your soul mate you won't get the same kind of reception from any of their family members," he chastises, and the triplets wisely keep their mouths shut.

"Now, I am still recovering. I think retiring is a good idea, Cole. I want to greet my kingdom tomorrow at full strength. Please have some enarac fruit brought to my suite for Fiona."

"Ah, what about breaking the pendant so Tia can have the spell on her lifted?" I ask, because it's the one thing we haven't discussed.

"Yes. Once I have shared my existence with the nation, I will announce that I am stepping down as king and explain the situation to my people. I will break the pendant, releasing Tia from her grandfather's spell, and then we will need to call on the goddess to elect a new vampire king. Hopefully she will hear our plea."

"What? No! That is our family right. The goddess selected us to rule over the vampires," Jacob argues, but my father shakes his head.

"No, Jacob. It would be selfish of me to hold onto it and make your sister suffer. It was fucking ingenious of Chen to tie her spell to the pendant. I'm almost certain he thought I—or you if you ever found out—would reject her as opposed to breaking it. I think he wanted to see her suffer even more."

The fury in Jacob's eyes softens as he looks at his new sister who is biting her lip with worry. I know there is no way they would rather remain as the ruling family than help out their newly discovered sister. The guys are a lot of things, but selfish is not one of them—or not with their family at least.

"So be it. At least that should stop the parade of women trying to get us to invite them into our beds," Jett says, running his hand through his hair and making it stick up at all angles.

"Thank you. I know how much you are all giving up. I'm not sure how I'll ever be able to repay you," Tia says, and we can all hear how grateful she is.

"Nonsense." Jeremiah comes over and pushes his father out of the way, gathering Tia up into a hug. "It's what we would do for any of our family. Plus, it wouldn't be right for you not to be at full strength. How can you fight back if you're being suppressed? It just wouldn't be fair." He pulls back and starts tickling her. She doubles over with laughter, unable to control her reaction at his sneak attack. "Look, boys, another giggling girl to add to our family. The little girls are going to be so happy to have a sister."

"What?" King Jarlen's eyes widen, and he suddenly looks sheepish. "Shit, I'm sorry. With everything that has happened, I didn't think to ask about your mother. How is she?"

"She's good. She and Abraham Sintax discovered they were mates a few years ago. She moved out of her suite here, and then they learned they were pregnant.

This time she gave birth to three girls. They are an adorable cyclone of terror when they come to visit. We turned Mom's old suite into their bedroom, and they regularly come for sleepovers and hang out with their favorite older brothers." Jacob smiles with affection, and it's nice to see. Maybe having little sisters has changed them for the better. Maybe they aren't as careless with girls' hearts now that they realize that some men will be breaking their sisters' hearts when they are older.

"Fabulous, we will have to have them over for dinner. I really want you and Lyndsey to meet," Jarlen says to Fiona. Tia's eyes just about bulge out of her head, and Fiona looks a little worried.

"Seriously, you want my mom to meet the other woman?" Tia sounds annoyed, and she pushes Jeremiah away. He still had his arm affectionately draped over her shoulders. I think he must realize how starved for affection she must have been growing up like she did. "No offense," she says, patting him on the hand, and he shrugs.

"None taken. Don't worry, it's not really that kind of situation," he assures her, and Jett jumps in.

"Not at all. As a king, Dad was expected to have an heir to carry on his line. Mom tells us they were nothing more than friends. They used each other for comfort, both wanting to find their true mates, but when Mom ended up pregnant, it was a huge surprise, so they decided it was a blessing from the goddess and they should take it."

"What do you mean by surprise?" Fiona asks, curious now.

"Having a child with someone other than your mate is rare," Jarlen answers.

"Thank goodness, considering how promiscuous we are while trying to find our mates. Otherwise, there would be hundreds of little vampire children running around from unmated relationships." Cole rolls his eyes but looks at the triplets when he says this.

"But it does happen on occasion. All children are loved here in the vampire realm. What humans do to their children is barbaric, and that would never happen here." Jett shakes his head, and Tia frowns at him.

"Yet human blood trafficking is acceptable?"

Jett straightens up. "No, of course not, and when we find Silvan and the rest of the people responsible, they will be put to death," he replies fiercely, and all the other men in the room nod their heads.

"Well, I would start looking at your portal guards and operators, because one of them had to have turned off the alarm every time a human was brought through. Someone had to be operating the portal on this side to send the vamps through who came back with humans," I tell them, and Cole scowls.

"I will get started right away. I can't believe this was happening under my nose." Cole is the head of security for the palace, so this is truly unsettling for him to hear.

I stand up because I can see that Tia is starting to fade. It's been a long day, and she needs to eat and get some rest before she goes through her awakening tomorrow. "I'm going to show Tia to one of the guest rooms and order her some food. It has been a long day."

"Make sure you show her to a guest room and not

yours," Jacob growls, and as one, Tia and I flip him off. Everyone chuckles.

"Leave them be. Thank you, Lucas. I can't tell you how much it means to me that you are looking after my girl. Sleep well, my princess, and tomorrow is going to be an exciting day for you." Jarlen gives Tia another hug, and so does Fiona.

The boys all wave goodbye, and I practically drag her out of the room. There is a back staircase that leads up to the royal accommodation wing. This is where the royal family and special guests sleep. I have a permanent suite here. The other accommodation wing in the palace houses all the staff, ministers, and advisors.

"What's the difference between a vampire awakening and a vampire mating?" Tia asks as we mount the steps hand in hand. "Because they seem to have the same outcome."

"They are two different potions given to us by our goddess. One of them triggers the latent vampire genes in our children, and the other rewrites the genetics of the nonvampire so that they can drink blood and have the same traits as a vampire. I hear it is more painful to transition from nonvampire to vampire, whereas your vampire awakening shouldn't be painful at all. Both are sexual experiences, and both involve blood. A mating requires the couple to exchange blood and invoke certain words to trigger the bond. An awakening only requires the vampire to take blood, and there are no ritual words."

"So I will only drink from you? You won't need to drink from me during my awakening?" Tia asks, and if

I'm not mistaken, there is a hint of disappointment in her voice.

I stop and push her up against the balustrade. Her eyes widen, and I hear her heart rate quicken in excitement. The air fills with the lush smell of her desire, and my fangs throb with need. I can't wait for tomorrow. I'm almost tempted to beg her to join me in my room tonight, but I won't. I will let her awakening be our first time, making it special and memorable.

"Oh no, my sweet witch. If you would like me to take your blood as well, I would be more than happy to do so. You are delicious," I tell her, running my nose up the length of her neck. I watch as goosebumps break out across her skin, and she shivers in anticipation. She's so responsive, I love it. "And I can't wait to taste everything else on you as well."

Before she can answer, I take her mouth with mine. I just need a quick sample to tide me over until morning. When her flavor hits my taste buds, my knees just about buckle. Her arms twine around my neck as I haul her closer to my body. Our tongues meet in a vicious fight for dominance. I knew this witch wouldn't be a wilting flower, she's too independent for that, but it will be fun to tame her.

I'm breathless with desire when I pull away. She is panting, and she chases my mouth with hers before she shakes her head.

"Holy cow," she mutters as she stares at me. "Is it always like that?"

"Never," I answer honestly, and her smile is blinding. "Come on. If I don't take you to your room, I'm likely to turn you around and bend you over here, and I want our first time to be special," I tell her, grabbing her hand and dragging her the rest of the way up the staircase.

"Rain check," she says, and when I look over my shoulder, she's smiling.

"Absolutely," I promise, adjusting my cock with my other hand. I hope we don't run into anyone else on the stairs.

CHAPTER
Fifteen

Tia

Lucas guides me to my room and shows me how to order food from the room service menu before he gives me another kiss that leaves me wanting and hurries away. I'd take offense at how quickly he left if I hadn't seen how hard he was in his jeans. Instead, I just feel a sense of satisfaction and anticipation. As nervous as I am for my vampire awakening, I'm ready to see what my magic can do once the spell has been broken.

I'm thrilled to find that my suite looks exactly like what I thought a room in a medieval castle would look like. There's a huge canopy bed on the back wall with a curtain-covered window on each side of it. Opposite the bed is a large fireplace, and around the fireplace is a small sitting area. There is a door on the opposite side of the entrance, and when I poke my head in, I find a dressing room with hanging space and a makeup vanity. Beyond that is a bathroom with an amazing clawfoot tub, a waterfall shower, and a separate toilet. The bathtub sits in front of a large window, which I'm assuming has some kind of tint over it for privacy, but who knows? Vampires seem open about their sexuality, so maybe voyeurism is a thing and they don't care if anyone sees them bathing.

My stomach rumbles, so I head back into the bedroom and look at the room service menu. Before Lucas left, he explained some of the dishes to me. Like Earth, their meat is predominantly chicken, beef, and pork, though they have a couple of unknown species on there as well. I stick to what I know best and order pan seared chicken with a creamy mushroom sauce, mashed potatoes, and steamed veggies. The voice on the other end tells me it will take about forty minutes, so while I wait, I'm going to take a bath. I want to try out some of the amazing smelling products that were lined up on the shelf.

Shit! I don't have anything to wear. I left my suitcase on Earth. Mom doesn't have anything either. We can't very well meet my father's court in our normal clothes, can we? Do they dress formally here? The triplets were wearing dress pants with casual button-down shirts. A knock on my door has me flinching. Hopefully it's someone I know who can help me with my problem.

Crossing the room, I open the door to find my mother and father on the other side. "Ah, good, you are here. Are you finding everything okay?" my father asks as I wave them into my room.

"Yes. Lucas showed me around and explained how to order food. I was just going to take a bath while I waited," I tell them as my mother walks into my bathroom and closet.

"I don't blame you. This bath is amazing," she calls, and my father chuckles.

I bite my lip, wondering if I should ask him this question or not. I mean, he's the king, so there are probably better people to ask.

"What's wrong, Tia?" His eagle eye sight catches my concern.

"I didn't bring anything with me. I noticed a robe on the back of the wardrobe door, but I can't very well wander around in that. Is there some place where I can get some clothes?"

"Oh, me too. I hadn't thought about that. Everything happened so fast, and I didn't think to pack a bag." My mother returns from exploring. She's holding a little jar of something in her hand. "This is from Scrubs and Suds." She holds out a familiar jar with a logo of a little yellow rubber duck wearing a witch's hat. "Why do you have these in the castle?"

My father looks confused and shrugs. "I have no idea what that is."

"It's one of the stores owned by Mom's fellow coven member, Denise Shelly," I explain, and his confusion clears.

"I guess maybe the boys must have ordered some to supply the castle, or maybe one of the people did."

"Well, that is very kind of them." My mom places the jar to the side.

"Anyway, I can solve your clothing dilemma

myself if things haven't changed that much in twenty-five years." My father takes my mother's hand and leads us both back into the closet, where he looks around before smiling. "Ah, no, it's still the same. That's a relief. This is a fae mirror." He points to the large, ornate, full-length mirror that stands off to one side. "All the rooms on this side of the castle have them. All you have to do is stand in front of it and imagine what you would like to wear." He does that, and suddenly he's no longer wearing the jeans and shirt he was in, but a pair of black dress pants and a blood-red tunic that has some fancy gold decorative features on it. He turns around and beams at our surprise. "Cool, huh?"

"Very cool," I squeal, dying to try it out now.

"And if you want to keep the outfit, just take it off and hang it up in here before standing in front of the mirror again, otherwise it will disappear and get replaced like mine did. I've been wearing those same clothes for twenty-five years. I don't care if I never see them again." He shudders before holding out his hand for my mother. "Shall we go, dear, and let Tia have her bath?"

"Yes. Bye, my love. Have fun creating outfits." My mother gives me a big hug and a kiss. "I'm so proud of how you are handling all this. I know it can't be easy," she whispers in my ear. "Tomorrow is your vampire awakening. When you get yourself all balanced out, we will finally sit down and talk. I want to hear about everything I missed out on, okay? I know I can never make up for what your grandfather did to you, but I am going to try my hardest for the rest of my life."

"I love you, Mom. None of this is our fault, so stop blaming yourself."

"Agreed, no one is to blame but the people responsible, and they will pay with their lives." My father clenches his fist, and his eyes flash red.

"See? Dad will make everyone pay, and we will live happily ever after." I squeeze her hand, but out of the corner of my eye, I see my father's mouth drop open.

"What's wrong, dear?" Mom must have noticed his reaction too.

"She called me Dad." A tear runs down his cheek, and I feel them well up in my own eyes as well.

"I hope you don't mind," I say shyly, and he quickly shakes his head, swiping away the tear at the same time.

"No, not at all. I'm so fucking happy about it actually."

"Jarlen," my mother replies, scolding him for his language, but I can see she's teary too. I decide that I am going to embrace this new journey just like Ruby would, so I drop my mom's hand and step up to my father. He's a good head taller than me, and when I look up at him, he has to tilt his head down to meet my eyes.

I hadn't realized how tall he was until now. I frown. "How come I didn't get your height?"

He chuckles and looks at my mom. "You're pocket sized just like your mother. It's wonderful."

I reach my arms around him and rest my head on his chest. I don't say anything, but I feel his breath hitch before his arms come up quickly to embrace me. He hugs me close, and it feels good and right and just like what I thought a dad's hug would feel like.

"Right then, come on. Let's let Tia have her bath in peace and quiet." My mother has to drag my father away, but he eventually leaves, albeit reluctantly. I don't think he was all that keen on letting me out of his sight, but I promised him I would spend plenty of time with him over the next couple of days.

I lean against the closed door and hug myself. How can one's life change so drastically in less than twenty-four hours? Ruby is right. That spell may have had consequences, but for my mom and me, they have been nothing short of amazing. I'm so glad I let her convince me to come home. Now I need to make decisions about my life. I guess being a vampire is going to make having a career in the human world a little more problematic, but I'm going to worry about that another day. I'll get through my vampire awakening and Feast and Fireworks like I promised Lucas and go from there.

Lucas is another thing to consider. I'm giddy and nervous all at the same time, thinking about what he's going to do to me tomorrow to help with my vampire awakening. He didn't go into much detail, and I'm not expecting him to declare his undying love for me after, but I think maybe there is something between us, and I wouldn't mind sticking around and exploring that a little more. The thought of staying on Morbank is becoming more and more enticing, and someone is going to have to take over my grandfather's business. I fully expect him to be dead by this time tomorrow, and I won't shed one fucking tear. In fact, I may just have a glass of champagne or whatever the vampire realm equivalent is to celebrate.

Pushing off the door, I hurry back to the closet. I had

every intention of taking a bath, but my food can't be too far away, and I'd have to be dead not to want to play around with the special mirror.

I spent the night in my room, not wanting to venture out and run into anyone I didn't know. I eventually did take that bath after my food was delivered. The staff member looked incredibly curious as to who I was, but he was well trained and didn't ask any nosy questions as he laid out my meal and left. My food was amazing, and the bottle of wine I ordered with it was a relaxing accompaniment to my bath. I lay there and let the beautiful bath products calm and soothe my frazzled nervous senses. It was just what I needed. It was dark outside, but my room overlooks a garden, and there were lots of little lanterns illuminating pathways and ponds and cute little sitting areas.

I can't wait to be able to explore, both inside and out. Honestly, I can't believe I'm sleeping in an honest to goodness castle. It's so freaking exciting, and I might have done a little booty shake dance after a couple glasses of wine.

I created a dozen outfits for myself, and I discovered the mirror is also intuitive. I asked it for an outfit for a royal announcement, and it designed a dress that I never would have come up with in my wildest dreams. It is seriously fit for a princess, but I guess that's what I am. It has a white bodice that slowly darkens down my body until it turns blood red at the bottom, matching the jacket my father wore. Not only does it provide clothes, but it also produces accessories too. I have a pair of elbow-length white gloves on and a necklace that looks like it may have garnets and rubies in it, with matching earrings and a funky pair of chunky black heels to give me a little extra height. It also gave me a full range of makeup perfectly suited for my skin tone.

When my mom and dad knock on the door the next day, both of them are glowing. I don't even want to think about what they have been doing to make them look like they are the optimum of health. Instead, I concentrate on what we're wearing. I'm fully dressed in my princess outfit, and I know I did the right thing because my mom is wearing an outfit very similar to mine, but hers is completely blood red. My father's outfit is the same one he chose last night, but he is also wearing some medals on his chest as well as a sword at his side and a crown on his head. Around his neck is his king's pendant, which my brothers brought to him last night. My mother is also wearing a small tiara. They look like the perfect royal couple.

"Wow, Tia, you are beautiful, just like your mother." My dad beams at me and holds something out. "But my princess is missing her own tiara." It seems like it matches the jewelry I'm wearing, and it's a smaller version of my mother's. I'm going to go out on a limb and guess this king's royal colors are shades of red. It's kind of fitting, I guess. I allow him to place it on my head, and he offers us both his arms. We loop our arms through his, then we walk through the deserted hallways. My father points out the different rooms as we go by.

My three brothers and Cole all have rooms on this floor, while Mom and Dad have the whole floor above us. We stop at a final door, and my father knocks on it. When it opens, my mouth drops open in surprise.

Gone are the T-shirt, sneakers, and jeans, and in their place is an outfit much like the one my father is wearing, but his tunic is in royal blue, which makes his eyes look more silver than gray. He doesn't have any medals pinned to his chest, but there is a sword. Swoon. Be still my beating heart. I press a finger to the corner of my mouth to make sure I'm not actually drooling.

He bows his head to my mother and father before turning to me. "May I escort you to the throne room?" he asks politely.

I step out of my dad's hold and slip my hand through his proffered arm.

"Aren't we the luckiest men in the vampire realm, Lucas? We have the two prettiest women on our arms." My dad can barely contain his joy, and my mom looks at him with so much love and devotion. I want that.

"Yes indeed, sir." Lucas doesn't take his gaze away from me, and I can see all the heat and promise of what's to come. Now I'm just anxious to get this show on the road.

"And whether we still live in the palace or have to move to my family home on the edge of the city. They will still be my queen and my princess, and I couldn't be happier."

Dad's words remind me about the other things that need to happen before we can get to the good stuff, so I straighten my back and adopt my best blank face that would drive my grandfather nuts.

"Let's do this, and if the goddess doesn't decide to award your family another medallion, well, she really is missing out," Lucas remarks.

CHAPTER
Sixteen

Lucas

Tia and I precede the king and queen down the
stairs to the private meeting room behind the
throne room. I was expecting to find just the
triplets and Cole waiting, but the room is in an uproar.
There are a number of royal cabinet members in attendance, all demanding to know what the meaning of this
meeting is, and unfortunately, I recognize one of them.

When my father gave up his ambassador position in
the fae realm to my sister, he instead got a cozy position
on the royal advisory board. The board is basically just
a farce, because they don't do much advising. The
triplets are more than capable of running a realm after
spending fifty years learning from their father, but in
the older generations' eyes, they were still very young
for a ruling position. They probably wouldn't have
taken over as kings until they were at least one hundred
and fifty, and they are still seventy-five years short of

that number, so the board was elected. All they really do is meet, drink, eat, and gossip, and the triplets have been happy to let them do that as long as they stay out of the way. Occasionally, however, they try to influence things, such as the portal keeper's position.

I eye the room, trying to work out who has the most to gain from the blood farm, and as far as I can tell, it could be any one of them, including my own father.

"Lucas, what are you doing here? You were told you were not welcome in my home if you were not going to take on the role I groomed you for," my father sneers.

"Ah, but Father, I found something you lost, and I just thought I would return it to you," I sneer back. I can't stand him, and I always end up being reduced to a defensive young man who could never make his father happy no matter what my choices were.

"You? What could you have possibly found that I would want?"

"Well, maybe not what *you* want, but I'm sure the vampire nation will feel differently." Tia and I part dramatically, allowing the rest of the room to see who is behind us. The noise drops to utter silence, and several mouths drop open with shock and not some small amount of unease.

The king frowns and holds his arms wide. "Surely someone is happy to see me?" That breaks the silence, and within moments, he is surrounded by kiss-asses all hoping and praying they are not about to lose their cushy positions. Tia and I get pushed to the side, and Fiona quickly joins us, followed shortly by the triplets and Cole.

"Look at those vultures. They are less than useless,

but no doubt they are going to try and prove to my father that he should keep them as an advisory board," Jacob scoffs.

"What did he do before? Did he have a council?" Tia asks. Since her mother is going to make the vampire realm her home, I'm sure she wants to understand more about this world.

"Yes, but it consisted of the three of us and Cole. Originally, Cole's family was on it too, but that is not the case anymore for obvious reasons," Jett explains, and Cole grimaces, but Jeremiah slaps him on the back.

"Hey, none of that. It's not your fault they were assholes, though I can guarantee this lot is going to fight tooth and nail to keep their positions."

"Yeah, but I've already started digging into things, and if they are guilty of conspiring with Silvan, then they will wish they had never been born." Cole's fists are clenched as he makes that promise.

"Your dad is still an asshole I see," Jacob comments, and I shrug.

"I hadn't expected him to change."

"We didn't realize he banished you from the realm." Jacob stares at me, and anyone with any sense would be scared, but these guys were—are my best friends, so they don't scare me at all.

"What can I say, he said he would make things difficult for you if I didn't leave. I'm not sad. I like my life in Morbank. I've missed you, but I never wanted to be involved in all the hustling and dealing that came with politics."

Tia's giggle is music to my ears and brings everyone's attention to her. "So you chose to become the mayor of a small town instead? There's more drama and politics there than there would ever be here."

I run my hand through my hair and smile at her a little ruefully. "It's really hard to say no to Pru when she sets her mind to something."

"You're not wrong." Fiona smiles. "Now I'm going to go see if I can rescue my mate. He seems to be a little overwhelmed." She wades her way through the crowd surrounding the king, and I see her zap people here and there when they won't allow her through. The one person who turned and hissed at her found their mouth quickly sewn magically shut—that got some attention. We watch on with amusement as Jarlen introduces his mate.

"Man, we thought you were mad at us because of Nettie," Jett says, his blue eyes narrowing, and I start to deny it, but Tia elbows me.

"Well, I was partly. You three could see how she felt for you, and yet none of you gave her the time of day. You'd basically pat her on her head and send her on her way while parading hundreds of women in front of her. I know it's not your fault she had a crush, but you could have spoken to her about it. Instead, she took my father's position with the fae, and I haven't heard from her in months except for an occasional text message assuring me she's fine."

The three triplets exchange a glance, and Jeremiah blows out a big sigh. "We didn't want her to choose."

Tia asks the question that was on the tip of my tongue. "Huh?"

"She would have picked one of us over the other two, and that wouldn't have been good. We agreed we'd rather be unhappy without her than see one of the three of us happy with her. It would have been worse if she had been one of our mates."

"Well, that's just stupid." Tia rolls her eyes. "Why couldn't she have had all of you?"

"That's not how it works. Vampires only have one mate," Jacob argues, and Cole frowns.

"Ah, no. That's not how it works. Or maybe it's become like that here in the city, but out in the villages, it's common to find polyamorous pairings."

"What do you mean?"

"Well, there is another ritual after the vampire awakening that can tell the newly awakened vampire how many mates they will have. It marks them with a small symbol on the inside of their elbow. Their mates will have a matching symbol."

"Why isn't that done here in the city? Why don't we know about it?" I ask, and Cole shrugs.

"You know what it's like. Things come in and out of fashion, and we have such long lives that things are forgotten. You also have to do the ritual for it to happen, otherwise you're left flailing in the dark."

"How do you know about this?" I ask him, and he rolls the sleeve of his black tunic back and holds out his arm. On the inside of his arm is a tiny quill with a pot of ink.

"I have friends in one of the villages. I went there for a mating celebration and discovered it. I went through the ritual."

"Is that a little pot of ink and a quill?" Tia asks, leaning closer, and he nods. "Have you found anyone that matches it yet?"

"No, and because of the lack of people doing the ritual in the city, it's probably unlikely that I will either."

I see sadness in Tia's eyes when Cole says this.

"I think I will speak to my father about making it a requirement to do the ritual after their awakening. It's not fair for the people out there who are missing their perfect match," she says, sounding determined.

"But that's taking away free will, and we don't like to do that," Jacob cautions her, and I see her shoulders sag. "But maybe we can make the possibility well known again and give people the option. I'm sure there aren't many who would say no."

Tia beams at Jacob, and I can tell she already has these guys wrapped around her little finger. It's kind of cute to be honest.

"Come, my friends, let's go announce my return to the rest of the nation, shall we?" Jarlen speaks loudly over everyone else, putting an instant stop to the noise. The council files out neatly, leaving us to follow behind them. My father stops in front of me as he passes by.

"You could have shown loyalty to your family and advised me of the king's return so we weren't blind-sided," he hisses, and I just stare blankly back at him.

"Yes, because you've been so loyal to me. Thanks, but no thanks."

"You'll pay for this, you'll see," he threatens, but I just ignore him. I don't have the time, nor do I want to waste my breath. My father will hear and see what he wants to.

Once again, I offer Tia my arm, and my father sneers

down at her. "Found yourself a witch to fuck? And one without much power either. How pathetic."

Tia starts to spark next to me. I worry that they are going to burn me, but instead, they just tickle. "Jesus, he sounds just like my grandfather. I guess earth doesn't have a monopoly on bigoted assholes," Tia remarks conversationally.

"Take a very close look at her, Father. Does she look like someone we know? Someone who has just returned to us? I would be very careful who you say those racist words to, because you may just find yourself in the dungeon for insulting the king's daughter." I get a thrill when my father looks between Tia, the king, and the queen and pales slightly. "Maybe you should just run along so you don't end up permanently staked," I suggest none too kindly.

My father whirls and marches off, and Tia sighs. "I'm sorry your dad's a dick."

"Me too, but my mom's lovely. I can't wait to introduce you to her."

The triplets lead the procession into the throne room. Their three seats are on a high platform with the receiving room stretched out beyond it. We enter from behind so no one can see the king yet, though I have no doubt there will be an uproar when his return is finally announced. The receiving room is filled with vampires chatting while they wait, so there is a loud hum that drops to silence as the triplets appear, the council already seated to the side of the raised platform.

I can see cameras situated throughout the room. This is being broadcast live to the entire realm. I didn't think it was a good idea, because it's going to tip off the blood farmers about Jarlen's return, but he wanted them to be scared. He hopes they will fuck up.

"Vampires, we are here to announce some glorious news," Jeremiah announces, spreading his hands wide. "My father, the king, has returned to us." Almost as one, the room gasps with shock. "I'm sure you will all be as thrilled as we are to know he is alive and well, and he has found his queen. Please put your hands together for King Jarlen and his mate, Queen Fiona."

I watch from the side as Jarlen and Fiona step regally forward, and the crowd goes wild. Fiona looks a little like a deer caught in the headlights with how enthusiastic the vampires are, but she smiles shyly and waves when King Jarlen does.

The cheers go on for at least five minutes before the king waves his arm for silence. "Thank you, my friends. It has been quite an adventure, and while I won't go into details about where I have been at the moment, I will have an official announcement released regarding my absence. As my son said, I did find my mate in the human realm, but I also have a daughter. Please welcome Princess Tia." He gestures Tia forward, and I give her a little push.

When she joins her parents on stage, there is a moment of silence before the cheers resume. Most seem happy for King Jarlen and not pissed like my father.

"Yes, and while I am thrilled to have them here with me and I can't wait to show them around our great nation, I am also sad to announce that because of a spell placed on my beautiful daughter, I am going to break the king's pendant today. The malicious spell has been attached to the pendant, and unless I break it, she will not be able to access her magic. While I adore being king to you wonderful people, I want my family's happiness more, and once I break the pendant, I expect the goddess to select a new ruling family."

Again, the noise is immense, but this time it's with shouts of outrage and dismay. I can't help but look over to the council. My father seems gleeful, as do a few other members. I must ask Cole to include them in his investigation in case he hasn't out of respect for me. I have absolutely no loyalty to him and his cronies.

Again, Jarlen waves for silence. "I, too, am sad at this outcome, but I will do anything for my newly reunited family. I would like you all to bear witness to this so that no one can dispute whom the goddess selects."

The crowd falls silent as Jarlen removes the pendant from his neck and places it on the floor at his feet. The sound of him removing his sword from its sheath is loud and reverberates through the entire hall. He lifts it high above his head, and then he pierces the amulet, cracking it in half. Tia screams and her back bows, and I jump forward just in time to catch her as she collapses. Jarlen drops his sword as the medallion starts to bleed, and so does Tia, a dark stain blooming on her dress in the middle of her chest.

"What have I done?" he mutters as Fiona drops to her knees next to us, grabbing her hand.

"What do we do?" I ask her, and she shakes her head, staring helplessly at her daughter.

"I don't know. I didn't expect that to happen at all."

The crowd whispers and pushes closer so they can see what is happening. The scent of Tia's blood perfumes the air, and I can see more than one vampire's fangs extend.

Suddenly, the light shining through the huge skylight above us starts to darken to a red haze, throwing the land into a blood red twilight. A figure begins to appear before us. At first, it's a shadowy, glittery cloud, but then it slowly becomes solid.

"The goddess," Jarlen whispers and falls to his knees, bowing his head, and the rest of the vampires follow suit. Even the council members drop to the ground.

The goddess is an ethereal beauty, with long red hair that falls around her naked body. Her fangs stick out over her lips, and her eyes glow a deadly red as she gazes around the room.

"Rise, King Jarlen. I respect your sacrifice for your daughter. That spell never should have been attached to such an object. It is my wish for you to continue to rule over the vampire realm, for only a king who is willing to give up everything for his family is worthy of such a task." The goddess's voice echoes throughout the room, and her power practically vibrates through my body, making my fangs ache.

Suddenly, the pendant appears whole once more in her hand. She places it over the king's head and bows her own to him. "Rule well and long, Jarlen, and I am happy with how your sons ruled while you were incapacitated. They will be worthy rulers to replace you once you decide to step down. When that happens, the pendant will split into three."

The goddess turns to Fiona and grasps her shoulders before leaning in and placing a kiss on her forehead. "You have my blessings too, Fiona Blackwell. Be a kind and just queen for the vampires."

She turns her heavy gaze to me and Tia, whose chest continues to ooze blood. "What happened to the young princess was unacceptable. Dark magic was outlawed for a reason. She will survive and will be stronger for it, but only her vampire awakening will save her now. She needs vampire regenerative healing to mend the magical wound. Go now, Lord Lucas, otherwise your mate may not survive."

My soul rejoices at hearing the goddess confirm that Tia is indeed my mate, but I'm also flooded with panic. She can't die before we've even begun to start our lives together.

Fiona gasps before starting to sob, and Jarlen drops to his knees to comfort her. "Go, Lucas. Save my girl."

The goddess waves a hand, and a blood-red light that I remember from my own awakening washes over Tia. "She will not need the ritual now, but when she wakes, her hunger will be fierce. Go now, Lord Lucas, hurry."

I pick Tia up and race her through the crowd that parts for us. The awakening rooms are on the other side of the castle, far away from any other rooms so nobody is disturbed. I only hope I can get there in time to save my mate.

CHAPTER
Seventeen

Tia

Once I regain consciousness, the pain in my chest becomes excruciating. I moan, and my head flops to the side as I try to look around. I'm being jostled, and we're moving too fast for me to see, so I squeeze my eyes shut again so I don't vomit.

"Hang on, baby. I've got you. The goddess said you would be okay, but she triggered your awakening. Your body is going to go through some changes as your vamp DNA comes online." That's Lucas's voice, so I'm assuming he's the one carrying me. Goddess?

I try to grab my chest where it's most painful, but I can't get my arms to cooperate, and then another sensation starts to fill my body. It's kind of like the feeling of pins and needles, but it washes through my whole body until every single nerve feels like it's on fire. Holy fuck, I thought Lucas said that an awakening didn't hurt. This is unbearable.

I try to scream, but my lips are locked, and all I can do is breathe heavily through my nose as my body completely stiffens up.

I hear a door bang open somewhere, and suddenly I'm no longer in Lucas's arms but on a soft surface, and he's brushing my hair back from my face and removing the jewels from my body. "The pain only lasts a moment. It should be gone shortly, and then you're going to start to feel hungry. The last thing that will happen is your fangs will click into place, and then you will be driven by instinct to bite me. Just go with it. You need the blood to kick-start your regenerative abilities to fix the wound in your chest. Drink as much as you need. I spent all night last night drinking blood to accommodate you. It's rather uncomfortable for me, so you will be doing me a favor," he explains as I feel the heaviness of my jewelry leave my body.

The painful tingles start to fade away, and a rush of soothing warmth replaces them, followed by an empty pang of need inside my stomach as well as throbbing need farther down. I moan as I realize how incredibly hungry and horny I am. I wiggle my fingers as feeling and movement return to my body. I slap my hand over my mouth as a profound ache makes me want to scream out loud, but I clamp my teeth together, not wanting to let the sound escape. I learned not to break with Grandfather, and I will not show Lucas how much pain I'm in.

"Aww, baby, it's okay, that will be your fangs. Just scream, I remember how much it hurt."

I can't respond because my eyes roll back in my head as my two top teeth lengthen and pierce my bottom lip. I pull my hand away and blink in shock. When I look up at Lucas, he's leaning over me and smiling, his own fangs showing, along with an incredible hunger in his eyes.

"There they are. Fuck, that's sexy," he growls and shifts uncomfortably.

Just like that, all the pain disappears, including the throb in my chest where I literally felt my father's sword pierce me the moment he stabbed the medallion. I scramble around to remove my dress, and when Lucas sees what I'm trying to do, he grabs either side of my bodice with his hands and tears it apart.

"Holy shit!" I exclaim as my dress parts and my breasts pop out, no longer contained by the material. I didn't need a bra with the built-in corset, and now my rock-hard nipples are on display, but Lucas doesn't look upset about it.

Looking down, I notice that my chest is no longer bleeding, and the wound seems to be knitting itself back together. I run my finger over the closing wound, mesmerized by what's happening.

Once it closes, all that remains is soft, scar free skin. I look up at Lucas in amazement, but then a red haze washes over my vision, and I start to growl as I scramble to my knees, untangling myself from my ruined dress and discarding it to the side, leaving me in just my panties. I don't feel self-conscious at all though, and Lucas looks at me like I am the most delicious dessert on the planet and he can't wait to take a bite. Before I can stop myself, I wave my hand, and his clothing disappears.

He gasps and looks down at his naked body. "Your magic works."

"You have no idea." I shake my head, my body practically vibrating with power. "I feel like I could rule the world," I tell him, and he chuckles.

"Well, how about you start small and rule this bedroom?" he suggests gently like he's talking to a wounded lion, and I guess, to him, that's how I could seem.

"How about you lie down on that bed so that I don't maul you?" I retort, the urge to pounce riding me hard.

He slowly slides his body onto the bed and shuffles back so he's leaning against the headboard. His whole body is displayed for me, and his long, thick cock stands at attention, begging for me to take it into my mouth. It's weeping precum, and I just want to run my tongue over it and catch every drop. Just as I think that, I find myself kneeling between his legs.

His eyes widen in surprise, and he blinks in shock. "Shit, you're fast."

I reach out to touch it, and he snaps a hand out so fast it leaves me blinking.

"Gently. Your strength will be great. It settles into place, but it's why we use blood consorts. They are specially imbued with extra strength to handle a newly awakened vampire. I really like my dick, so let's not accidentally rip it off. Normally, I would have taken the same potion as the consorts, but there wasn't time."

I sit back on my heels, afraid to touch him now, but he shakes his head. "Just go easy, and you will be fine."

I wish he had the potion so I didn't have to worry about my strength. I no sooner think this before a small cup appears on the side table next to the bed.

"Is that what I think it is?" Lucas asks, picking up the glass and sniffing it. "Holy shit, it is. How did you do that?" He throws back the potion, grimacing slightly as I shrug.

"Apparently my witch powers are pretty strong at the moment too."

No longer worried, I settle down and lick a long line up the length of his cock. He moans, and the cup drops onto the floor as his head falls backward.

"Fuck, that feels good." He threads his fingers through my hair and gently holds my head as I lick and suck my way up and down his thick length. I lightly scrape my fangs across his thigh, but an overriding urge to bite down hits me, and I sink them deep into his femoral artery. He shouts and thrusts up as I remove my fangs and latch my lips onto the two holes. His blood floods my mouth, and although I thought I'd be grossed out, I'm not. I thought it would taste coppery, but it's delicious, like strawberries and wine, and I take huge gulps of it as he writhes beneath me.

"Fuck, Tia!" he shouts, and I feel a hot liquid run over my hand that's stroking his dick.

I can't stop drinking, but his fingers push between my lips, breaking the suction I have on his leg. He grabs me and hauls me up his body, slamming his mouth onto mine and kissing me. Lucas tastes his own blood in my mouth as he swirls his tongue around mine.

I straddle his body and grind down, wanting to be filled by his thick cock. He pulls away, and his eyes flash red. I wonder briefly if mine are doing the same as he growls, "Next time I come, I want to be buried deep inside your cunt."

Mayor Sharpe has a dirty mouth, and I am so here for it. Before I can respond, he thrusts his dick deep, and I scream, unprepared for the intrusion despite how wet I am. He's thick, and it takes him a couple of thrusts before he's buried deep, but the pain just adds to the pleasure. I throw my head back and moan loudly, and he rakes his fangs over my nipple, my skin prickling with anticipation.

"Do it," I demand, and he sinks his fangs into my skin. I hear the pop as they go in, and then he removes them, surrounding the holes with his lips and drinking deeply. It triggers my first orgasm, and I try to move on his cock, but he holds me in his vicelike grip, and all I can do is stay there, my pussy rippling around the thick intrusion when all I want to do is ride him like a pony.

"Now we're even. That's a good start. I like to give as good as I get," he says, pulling back. A trickle of blood runs down my skin from the punctures. His mouth is bloody, his eyes are red, and he looks feral, but I've never seen anything sexier. "Look at how pretty you are painted in blood," he says as we watch the ribbon of red flow down my body and pool where we are joined.

He removes one hand from my hip and uses it to paint blood all over me. I should be freaked out, but I'm even more turned on. He lifts me slightly, and I watch as my blood circles his dick, and he growls with satisfaction. He starts to thrust up, holding me slightly aloft, and I watch as his dick becomes coated in the blood that I now know is also lining the inside of my pussy, making me even slipperier.

He lowers me back down but continues to roll his hips, and my breathing picks up once more as he hits all the right spots inside me. He leans in and runs his tongue over the fang wound on my nipple, sealing it before chasing all the blood around it. I watch with fascination, dying to do the same thing to his chest. I want to mix our blood together, and he must see my desire in my eyes.

"I can see how much you want to bite me, but the next time you do, we're going to bite together, and that will activate our mating. Are you sure that's what you want?" he asks, lifting my chin so I meet his gaze.

I search my emotions for any hesitation and find none. Despite having known this man for less than twenty-four hours, I'm ready to spend the rest of my long, extended life with him. He must mistake my silence for hesitation, because he pulls his finger away and stops thrusting, but I grab his chin and make him look at me.

"Abso-fucking-lutely. Now bite me, damn it." I lean in and sink my fangs into his chest. He shouts and starts to fuck me furiously as I watch his blood dribble down his chest and mix with mine. Leaning in, I seal my mouth to his skin and drink. My eyes roll back in my head, and my orgasm isn't far off despite him not biting me yet. I feel him lift my arm and bite down in the crease of my elbow, and as he starts to suck, I feel something click into place between us. His thoughts flood mine, and I sense how he feels—all the built-up love and affection and desire he has for me. My orgasm explodes through me, making every nerve in my body sing as everything aligns, our hearts, souls, and blood joining forever more. Throwing my head back, I scream as I ride his cock hard, bouncing up and down and milking it for every drop of cum he has. I want to feel him deep inside me. He grunts and groans as he swallows down mouthfuls of my blood.

We fuck and drink from one another for hours. My thirst seems unending, and my pussy never seems to be satisfied. Lucas takes me in every position possible, and I even beg him to fuck my ass, which I've never done, but being surrounded by his large frame as his cock slowly slides in and out of my dark channel feels incredible, and my orgasm is different from all the others, especially because he found an attachment that slid over his dick that fucks my pussy at the same time. Being double penetrated is unlike anything I've ever felt before, and I will be bringing that little toy home with us for sure.

Eventually, we come up for air, and we shower and eat something, but soon enough, the bloodlust takes over, and we start all over again. Thank goodness for vampire stamina, because I'm pretty sure this would kill a normal person, but if it did, what a way to go.

CHAPTER
Eighteen

Lucas

Tia and I are lost in a sex haze for the next few days, solidifying her vampire awakening and celebrating our mating. Eventually, though, we have to leave our nest, and Fiona must be worried and impatient, because by the third evening, there is a knock at the awakening room door. Tia is fast asleep, so I climb out of bed, where I had been wrapped around her, and grab a towel to drape around my waist.

Going over to the door, I crack it open to find Tia's mother standing there, gnawing on her lip with her front teeth.

"I'm sorry. Jarlen told me to wait, but I just couldn't. I need to know that my baby is okay," she explains.

I grimace and look down at my half naked body. "Sorry, I have no clothes. Tia's magic got rid of the ones

I was wearing, and we don't have spelled mirrors in here," I tell her, and a small smile creeps across her face as she waves her hand. I'm instantly clothed in sweatpants and a soft hoodie, so I throw the towel to the side.

"So her magic works?" she asks, trying to look around me.

I block the way, because the room is a mess, and there are a few blood splatters from where we got a bit rough a couple of times. I don't want to freak her out, though I'm sure she and Jarlen have had the same experiences.

"She's so strong, it's ridiculous," I reply, and she beams.

"It's probably because it's been bottled for so long and it's just happy to be free. Magic is slightly sentient like that. It will settle much like her vampire strength and senses. The other reason I woke you is because Jarlen is itching to go after the blood farm. Cole has had no luck in locating them yet, but I remembered you had a victim's top. I'd like to do a locator spell for her."

"Yeah, of course. It's in my suite. When Tia wakes up, I'll grab it for you. I don't really want to leave her alone," I say, but then I hear a voice call out.

"I'm awake. Tell Mom we'll meet her in the lounge behind the throne room in an hour."

"Is that okay?" I ask the queen, and she smiles.

"Yes, of course, that sounds good. I'll let the others know." Fiona disappears in a flash, using her vampire speed, and I close the door before stalking back to the bed. Tia is sitting there with a sheet covering her naked body, her hair looking well fucked and her eyelids heavy.

"Are you okay?" I ask her, sliding back into the bed and taking her into my arms. "Are you hungry? Do you need to feed?"

She shakes her head and slaps a hand over her mouth. "Morning breath," she explains when I raise a questioning eyebrow.

I chuckle. "Ah, my beautiful mate, morning breath doesn't bother me at all. Now give me that mouth." I push her hand away and kiss her deeply.

She moans and rolls on top of me, grinding against my rapidly hardening dick. She starts to pluck at my clothes, trying to remove them, so I grab her hands and pin them at her sides.

"Uh-uh. As much as I would like to do this, we really need to get up and shower. Finding those humans is a major priority, and I would be a bad mayor if I let my dick rule my decisions."

She pouts playfully but slides off me again, rolling from the bed and putting her hands on her hips. All her glorious, pale golden skin is on display, and her long, black hair tumbles over her shoulder.

"Fine, I guess you're right." She turns and sashays toward the bathroom, her pert ass swaying enticingly as I roll out of bed and strip off my sweats, hurrying after her.

"I guess we could be efficient and make use of our time in the shower."

Forty minutes later, after I thoroughly ravish my mate in the shower and feed her, Tia waves her hand and clothes us.

She looks down at her jeans and T-shirt. "Do I need to dress more formally than this?" she asks, and I shake my head.

"No, just for special occasions, though if we are going to look for the blood farm, then maybe wearing a soldier's uniform will be better, but we can change before we leave. Their uniforms are specially coated to be bullet and knife proof."

She looks around the room that we trashed and grimaces.

"Don't worry about it. It's normal, I promise. Someone will be in to clean up when we leave."

"I don't like the idea of leaving our blood lying around. I just got out of one spell, and I don't want anyone to get hold of any of this and use it against us."

My eyebrows jump in surprise. I hadn't ever thought about that.

She waves her hand, and blood droplets rise into the air, forming a big ball of blood. Tia then closes her hand, and the blood catches on fire and goes up in smoke, leaving no trace of it behind.

"Wow, you're really getting the hang of those powers," I tell her, and she grins and does a happy dance. It's so freaking adorable, I just want to strip her down and fuck her again, but I resist the urge.

"Yeah. It's natural. I just think about it, and it happens. You have no idea how I struggled just to produce a small flame in the past. This is like a firestorm in comparison." She sounds slightly giddy, but I know she's not going to turn power hungry. She's too humble for that.

"Come on, your family is waiting, and I'm sure your father is dying to put an end to this blood farm."

Tia wraps her arms around me and gives me a kiss. Before she can pull away, our bodies shimmer, and then there's a lurching sensation, and when we pull apart, we're standing in my bedroom in my suite.

I look down at her in shock. "You teleported us."

"Yes, I've always wanted to be able to. That was awesome."

"Ugh, now I know how you feel after I ran with you." I lean over, bracing my hands on my knees, and suck in a couple of breaths, praying for the nausea to ease. My mate just giggles at my pain. "Okay, I guess I deserve that, but warn a guy next time, okay?" I press a kiss to her forehead and grab the plastic encased shirt from my safe.

"Okay, think we can do that again, but to the reception room?" I ask her, and she grins, wrapping her arms around me and leaning her head against my chest.

"I love you," she murmurs, and we teleport again. I'm so distracted by her words that I don't even notice this time. She loves me, and I couldn't be happier about it.

"What the fuck are you grinning about?" an

annoyed voice says, and we step apart to find Jett staring at us, looking slightly grossed out.

"She loves me," I tell him, beaming, and he rolls his eyes, but I see he's struggling to keep his smile hidden.

"Well, good for you, but I'd appreciate it if you kept your hands PG when we're around. Nobody wants to see their baby sister being defiled."

"Oh leave them be, Jett. I remember what it was like for Fiona and me when we first mated. We couldn't keep our hands to ourselves." Jarlen snuggles into Fiona's neck, and she giggles, but this time all four of their children look slightly green. Cole and I chuckle.

"Okay, PDA is now banned." Jacob throws himself back into one of the sofas with a whiskey in his hand.

"Yes, agreed. Come on, Lucas, hand over the shirt. I feel like cracking heads." Jeremiah puts his hands together and stretches them out, and we hear his knuckles pop.

"I love you too," I whisper into Tia's ear before she pulls away, and then I offer the shirt to Fiona.

She untangles herself from the amorous king and pulls the shirt out of the plastic. "I need a map," she says, and Jacob stands up and leads us to another door off the side of the room. It leads to the war room. It hasn't been used in years, but it's kept clean. There is a huge map of the realm on a large table, which allows generals to plan battle strategies and troop positioning.

"Is this okay?" he asks, turning on the light and showing Fiona the table.

"That's perfect," she says, and we all follow them into the room.

Tia slips her hand into mine as we stand around the

table and watch Fiona work. She begins to chant, and a small ball of magic jumps out of the shirt and hovers above the table. It lingers in place for a moment before it seems to shudder and then shoot down onto the map, lighting up a section of it.

"That's the death forest," Cole says.

Tia snorts. "Of course it is. Where else would an evil organization have their lair?"

"It's where the trees that provided the wood that kills vampires used to grow. They were all destroyed many, many years ago. Now, nothing grows there, nor are there any buildings." Jacob sounds confused, and he looks at Fiona who shrugs.

"The magic says she is there, so I say we go and take a look."

"If my grandfather was working with one or more of your vampires, then what's to say that he didn't give them a concealment spell? When was the last time you went to this death forest?" Tia asks, and I squeeze her hand. That's a good question.

"No one has ventured there in years. It is off limits. We had a fae made repellent spell applied to the land back when we destroyed the forest. Master Alsorin cast it for us, and I trust him completely," Jarlen explains.

"Well, there are ways to undo such spells, so I say we check it out." Jett looks at Cole. "Have the assassin squad meet us there. We will investigate with a small group first. We don't want to spook anyone with a large army."

Cole nods and disappears in a flash.

"Shall we run or take the horses?" Jeremiah asks his father.

After her initial blood haze had worn off, I explained to Tia that, despite our modern conveniences and advanced technology, we still use horses and carriages for transport if we use any at all. We can run so fast that vehicles really aren't needed. Horses aren't either, but sometimes we don't want to run places.

"Tia and I can teleport us once Cole returns," Fiona offers, and Tia nods her head in agreement. "That way you have the element of surprise and stealth."

"That would be great. Thank you, Fiona." Jacob nods to his new stepmom.

It doesn't take Cole long to return, and while we wait, Jarlen orders us all to change into a soldier's uniform for extra protection. The leather-like material hugs our bodies, allowing freedom of movement while still protecting us against most common weapons. I just about swallow my tongue when I see my new mate in hers. She looks at me with the same kind of appreciation, and I kind of wish we could just go back to our room.

"What did I say?" Jacob smacks me on the back of the head, and I stumble forward before whirling around and snarling at him. Everyone else just laughs, and Tia puts a hand on his shoulder.

"Leave him be, Jacob. You will be the same when you find your mate." Jacob quiets down and looks at the crook of his elbow, which is covered by the uniform.

The three of them took the mate potion during Tia's awakening, and they all have the same mark, which really isn't surprising, but so far, a female bearing their mark hasn't come forward. The mate potion has become all the rage now, though, and people know what the triplets' mark looks like, so they'll find her eventually.

Cole arrives back from talking to the elite assassin squad, and within moments, we've gathered in a circle and linked hands, allowing Tia and Fiona to teleport the eight of us to the death forest.

Jett turns and vomits the moment we stop moving, and the other vampires groan. I've adjusted now and only feel a moment of disorientation, so I'm feeling quite smug about it.

"I'm running home," Jett grumbles as he wipes his mouth with the back of his hand.

Tia produces a bottle of water and hands it to him. He smiles gratefully at her and takes a swig, swirling it around in his mouth before spitting it out. He then drinks the rest, and she gets rid of the bottle.

"How long until the squad gets here?" Fiona asks, looking around and shivering before hugging herself. "There is dark magic at play here."

Tia shivers too, and she shakes her body like she's trying to rid herself of a tick. "It feels wrong. There is still a repellent spell here."

"Yes, but it doesn't feel like it's fae," Fiona says. "It feels like my dad's spell.

Tia sends out a stream of magic, much like Fiona did back on earth when we were looking for Chen's warehouse.

Sure enough, it hits something solid, and another large warehouse comes into view.

"Holy shit," Jeremiah murmurs, and Cole takes a step forward.

"Wait," I call to him and put out a hand, stopping

him. This time it's Fiona's magic that streams out, feeling for booby traps and other spells. One or two pop and fizzle out, becoming benign, and eventually she gives us the go-ahead to move forward.

We just make it to the door when the squad of ten assassin vampires arrive to back us up.

"Detain and capture anyone you can, but defend yourselves if you need to. I'd like to keep at least one vampire alive who can shed more light on the situation," Jarlen instructs then nods for Cole to kick down the door.

He does, and the assassins stream in and spread out. "Stay with me," I tell Tia, drawing my gun and holding it up, ready to defend us. Her body starts to spark, the fireworks staying close to her skin.

Jacob reaches out to touch them and yelps, pulling his hand back. "How come you can touch them?" he asks, sticking his injured finger in his mouth.

"Because he's my mate." Tia rolls her eyes at her brother, whose finger has already healed. "Didn't your mother tell you not to touch things?"

"Of course, but he never listened." Jeremiah pushes past us and follows the king and queen into the warehouse. A shout from inside has us hurrying after them. Fiona has thrown a ball of light onto the ceiling because there doesn't seem to be a light switch nearby. What the light illuminates is nothing short of distressing.

"Holy fuck," Tia murmurs as we take it all in.

We see row after row of plastic wrapped humans, hanging like sides of beef, with various tubes going into and out of the bag they are suspended in. Jarlen steps closer to one and examines it.

"They are alive," he says as we all move closer.

We can see the human's chest rising and falling. There is red tubing going into a keg next to the machinery, all of which looks like it's being used to keep the human alive so they can be milked.

One of the assassins returns to Cole. "The warehouse has been cleared. There is no one here, but there are still scents here, so they have only been gone an hour or so," he announces.

"Fuck." Cole runs his hand through his hair. "Somebody must have tipped them off."

"And we will find out who. Only us and a few select individuals knew that Fiona was going to do a locator spell. I trust everyone here, so I have a list to investigate when we return to the palace. But first things first, we need to get some medical teams out here right away and have them assess whether or not we can take the humans down and what needs to happen. That is our priority," Jarlen orders, and Cole moves away to speak to the rest of the assassins.

"This is a PR nightmare, but we've shut it down now, so hopefully the supranatural council won't get involved," Jett says, and Jacob shakes his head.

"I don't think we will be that lucky, but maybe they won't want it brought to the attention of the human authorities, so that may be our saving grace. That, and we need to produce those responsible."

"We will. The net is closing on them now, and when I find them, they will die," Tia's father promises, and I shiver as fear goes down my spine. I wouldn't want to be on the other end of Jarlen's fury.

Epilogue

Tia

I watch with pride as the fireworks light up the sky over the river on Morbank Island. People ooh and ahh as the Thanksgiving turkey I spelled into the burst twerks its bottom in time to the soundtrack. All around us, people twerk along with the deranged turkey, laughing and singing and having a blast. People flooded the island for this event. Tickets sold out within an hour of going on sale, and there was a waitlist a mile long. The stores were full throughout the day, with visitors trying to make the most of their trip before the main event in the evening. Although snow covers every surface of the island now, Main Street was cleared, tables were set up, and fires and heaters were placed everywhere to keep the patrons warm. The food was bountiful and delicious, and the fae mead flowed. Lucas's arm feels heavy around me, but I'm not uncomfortable. It's the opposite, really. I feel loved and cherished, and I am never going to get sick of his attentiveness.

The humans were removed from the farm, and after a week in the hospital in the fae realm, they were returned to their human lives with false memories. I felt a little dishonest when my father announced that, but when they explained that it was for both the vampire realm and the coven's protection, I agreed it had to happen. None of them are worse for wear, but a little added compulsion to stay away from strangers was added to their subconscious.

"Wow, Tia, those are even better than your grandpa's!" Ruby bounds up to us, followed by her boyfriend, Maddox.

"Hey, man, you did an amazing job with all of this." He greets Luca by shaking his hand before leaning in to give me a kiss on the cheek.

"I can't take much of the credit. Pru did most of this while we attended to some things in the vampire realm."

Although the coven knows what happened, we don't talk about it in public because you never know who is listening.

"So are you two living together now?" Ruby, the nosy bitch, asks. "Are you going to stay here, or are you moving to the vampire realm?" I can hear the trepidation in her tone. We've held off on telling anyone our decision because neither of us were sure what we wanted to do.

I exchange a glance with my mate, who gives me a small nod. "We will be staying here for now. The island needs us, and I can visit Mom and Dad whenever I want, thanks to the portal opening more regularly now that Regan's tours are such a hit," I reply.

"Regan's tours are so popular that he is booked out for over a year now and looking to employ more staff so they can run more than one at a time."

"Yes!" Ruby shouts and throws her arms around Lucas and me, giving us both a huge hug. "That's awesome. Alright, so Christmas, we need to think about that."

I frown and look over to the North Pole Christmas shop, which is still doing a roaring trade despite the lateness of the evening. "I didn't recognize anyone in there tonight. Where are the LaCroixs?"

Ruby's smile drops. "Mom said she spoke to them yesterday. They have been delayed in Germany. One of their suppliers is being difficult, so they weren't able to make it back in time."

"And Winter? Do we know where she is?" I ask, and she shakes her head, tears gathering in her eyes.

"No. Mom asked, and they had no idea. They haven't seen or spoken to her in months. They still had a fairly good relationship. She still bought all the stock for the store since she left the island, but when they hadn't heard from her, they had to go themselves. Even a locator spell fizzles out when they try to find her."

My heart skips a beat, and my hand tightens in Lucas's.

"That's weird. What could that mean?" Lucas asks, and us three witches exchange a loaded glance.

"It could mean she's dead," Maddox says solemnly.

Lucas mulls over the information. "What about in another realm? Would it do that if she wasn't on Earth?"

Ruby's frown disappears, and she looks hopeful. "You know, I think it probably would." She leaps in and smacks a kiss on my mate's lips. "You are a fucking genius, Mayor Sharpe. Come on." She drags away a bemused Maddox, who lifts a hand in farewell, and I chuckle at the stunned look on Lucas's face.

"Did she just kiss me?" he asks, sounding a little shaky.

"Yeah, you'll get used to it," I reply, chuckling. I'm not jealous in the least. My friend is crazy, and that's what I love about her. I have no doubt that Ruby will be able to find Winter, I just hope Lucas is ready to hold onto his socks, because it's likely to be an action-packed ride.

Thank you for reading!

I hope you enjoyed this book. It would be super awesome if you could leave a review wherever you bought it, because I'd love to hear what you thought of the story.

Acknowledgments

To Dazed Designs for the amazing cover

And of course Jess from Elemental Editing who made this a much neater book. You're the best, babe.

Also thank you to all my ARC readers who volunteered to read this.